DEAD GIRLS
AND OTHER STORIES

DEAD GIRLS

AND OTHER STORIES

EMILY GEMINDER

DZANC
BOOKS

5220 Dexter Ann Arbor Rd.
Ann Arbor, MI 48103
www.dzancbooks.org

Library of Congress Cataloging-in-Publication Data

Names: Geminder, Emily, 1986- author.
Title: Dead girls & other stories / Emily Geminder.
Other titles: Dead girls and other stories | Dead girls.
Description: First edition. | Ann Arbor, MI : Dzanc Books, 2017.
Identifiers: LCCN 2017003747
Subjects: LCSH: Dead--Fiction. | Spirits--Fiction. | Paranormal fiction. |
   GSAFD: Fantasy fiction.
Classification: LCC PS3607.E455 A6 2017 | DDC 813/.6--dc23
LC record available at https://lccn.loc.gov/2017003747

First US edition: October 2017
Interior design by Michelle Dotter

Stories in this collection appeared, sometimes in different form, in the following publications: "Houses" in *Mississippi Review* as "Are You on the Road to Salvation?"; "1-800-FAT-GIRL" in *American Short Fiction*; "Coming To" in *Prairie Schooner*; "Phnom Penh" in *New England Review* as "Phnom Penh 2012"; "Your Village Has Been Bombed" in *Witness*; "Choreograph" in *AGNI*.

Printed in the United States of America

10   9   8   7   6   5   4   3   2   1

CONTENTS

For Miles and Ari

It is not what they built. It is what they knocked down.
It is not the houses. It is the spaces in between the houses.
It is not the streets that exist. It is the streets that no longer exist.
It is not your memories which haunt you.
It is not what you have written down.
It is what you have forgotten, what you must forget.
What you must go on forgetting all your life.
And with any luck oblivion should discover a ritual.

—James Fenton, "A German Requiem"

HOUSES

Homeless: this is the game. Eskimo and me in the backseat. Eskimo and me inside blankets, sheets. At a rest stop, we pocket gummy worms, Milky Ways. We shoot like comets down the aisles, then disappear fast as light. Outside, on a picnic table, our mother sits smoking. Outside, our mother says, Let's go.

In the backseat, we pull blankets over our heads. Eskimo does the sign for *house*: hands flat like a roof, then walls. He likes to be inside. He likes to peer out. Every day, we build this house from scratch. I tell him, This is what it means to be homeless. You carry your house around inside you.

We're not homeless, says Mom, overhearing. We're between places. We're in between.

We keep driving: Eskimo between silences, Mom between cigarettes. Me: a too-tall girl between seventh and eighth grade.

We get a hotel room with two beds, and I build Eskimo a house on the floor between them. Mom smokes outside, then crawls in beside us and we all lay there breathing at once.

When Mom was pregnant, she dreamt she was giving birth to an Eskimo baby, and that's what Eskimo looked like when he came out: shock of black hair, squinty eyes. The watery thing that's supposed to break unbroken and shining like snow.

Look, Laney, said Mom, placing him in my arms. Our Eskimo baby.

Eskimo squinted and kept squinting like he was always looking past. He got another name, but Eskimo was the one that stuck.

Things stick to Eskimo. Like the houses. Like the signing. The speech therapist who used to come said it would one day turn into talking. She said, Downs kids know the words before they can say them.

But Eskimo's five now, and he still talks this way. In the back of the car, he does the sign for *pray*: two hands pressed together. He does it because it makes me laugh every time. I don't know why. Or he points a stubby finger at my forehead, like E.T.

I'm Elliott, I tell him, and you're E.T.

He signs back that *he's* Elliott and I'm E.T.

I shake my head. I've never met anyone more like E.T. in my entire life, I say.

The hotel rooms get smaller, and then we sleep in the car, windows partway down. It's summer. I point to stars and tell Eskimo how, far back and forever, people were drawing lines between them. How the right star could save you. How sailors used them to find the way home. Eskimo traces my hand with his finger. He does this sometimes.

On the highway, the wind blasts my hair. I think maybe we'll speed all the way to the ocean. Signs tell us: Forty miles from the birthplace of Ronald Reagan. Thirty miles from GHOST TOWN IN THE SKY. JESUS WANTS YOU TO PRAY, PRAY, PRAY. And: ARE YOU ON THE ROAD TO SALVATION?

There it is, says Mom. That's where we're going.

Where?

Salvation.

But the next day we turn around. We've made our point, says Mom. We've gotten far enough to come back.

What about Salvation?

Laney, that was a joke.

I can feel Eskimo watching my face. He presses his palms together, and I try to smile. I hadn't known this was what we were doing. I hadn't known we were coming back.

Back home, I'd been dreaming the same dream: our house was burning, and I had to get Eskimo out. Back home, I made lists. Ways of being saved. At home, sometimes things were okay.

Billy starts crying the minute we pull up the driveway. He makes us all sit down in the living room, and Eskimo's already crawling into his lap, signing *Dad*.

That will never happen again, Billy tells us, but most of all he looks at me. Never. Understand?

Okay, I say.

Ways of being saved:

By a fireman, from a burning house.

From terrorists, by presidential decree.

Stars, lifeboat at sea.

Eighth grade starts, and Salvation gets farther away. I try to explain it all to my best friend Maggie. How we took off in the middle of the night, how we slept in the car.

Like camping?

Sort of.

After school, we do our dance routine on Maggie's white shag carpet. "Hit Me Baby One More Time." We eat popcorn and watch Wrestlemania on her parents' waterbed. Sometimes I think Maggie's whole house is like one big waterbed, even the toilet seats plush and springy. The world could roll you around and around in this house, and nothing would ever happen to you.

On TV, the wrestlers keep trying to lay each other down in caskets. Maggie and her little brothers like Triple H, his muscles big and shiny as soup cans. I like the Undertaker, who looks ghostly and pale. Who looks like someone who's lost his shine.

He wears *eye*liner, says Maggie. And what kind of name is Undertaker, anyway?

Her brother chimes in: It's cause he can raise people from the dead.

Maggie shrugs. It's not like he's Jesus or something, she says.

Maggie is saved, which means she gets to talk about Jesus like she knows him. Like him and her talk all the time. The closest I ever got was one day on the swing set in Maggie's backyard. We were watching some carpenters up on the roof, and Maggie said: Jesus was a carpenter.

And right then, I swung my leg over the monkey bar and felt something between my legs—like sinking and rising all at once. It shuddered up through me, and for a second I understood.

Maggie's mother calls from downstairs. Maggie and her brothers have to get ready to leave. They go to a kind of Sunday school even when it's not Sunday.

We skid down the carpeted hall and into the kitchen, where Maggie's mother eyes me. Do you need a ride, Lane? she asks. But really she means: Why is your mother always late?

No, I tell her. It's okay. My mom will come.

So Maggie and her brothers shove into the minivan, and I'm left sitting on the porch. The house next door still has Halloween decorations up, cobwebs and a talking skull. When the cat walks by, the skull says, *I want your soul.*

I think again about the soft insides of Maggie's house. I know the fake plant where they hide the key. I decide to go back in and sit one more time on the springy toilet, but I wind up lying on the waterbed instead.

From being buried alive, at the very last minute.

By the Undertaker.

By Jesus on the cross.

I reach down and try to get the shuddery feeling I got that day on the monkey bars: the sinking that's also like rising. I think of Jesus reaching inside me and grasping my squirming red heart in his hand. It slips between his fingers with a little punctured *Oh.* Then it's the Undertaker pressing me down inside a casket: darkness and the taste of dirt.

When I look up, I see Maggie's father standing in the doorway.

How it is at night: like storm clouds, like natural disasters with names going down the alphabet. Catastrophic and then over and never again.

Sometimes Eskimo and me climb out onto the roof. Eskimo points to stars and I name them. I say: That one's the sign we saw, Ghost Town in the Sky. Over there is the birthplace of Ronald Reagan. I keep going. In the quiet, you can hear things. Knuckles, bones. Pucker sound the body makes when punched. You can hear it rising, up and up above the rooftops.

Sometimes it gets so dark, I have to touch my skin to see if I'm real. I grasp at my wrist. Kneecap, collarbone. A me-shaped connect-the-dots. Eskimo traces my hand with his finger, like he's writing me into the dark. I point at our neighbor's satellite dish and tell Eskimo how it's bouncing our signals into outer space, a sign or a flare.

In the mornings, we put on a whistling show of *everything's fine, just fine.* I look over at Eskimo, who flaps a sock in front of his face. Who occupies time in the full and uncut way I used to.

But lately it's like the storm has gotten inside me. Quiet makes my brain addled and jumpy. Bats and lightning lurch around inside my chest.

At night, after Eskimo's asleep in his plastic car bed, something pushes me out the door and I wander around the streets in the dark.

In the dark, you're nowhere, you're always in between. I walk all the way to the edge of town just to feel something.

Later I sneak back in and find Eskimo sitting at the top of the stairs. I tuck him back into his car bed, but in the morning, when I wake up, he's a small round ball curled against my spine.

Last year, in seventh grade, there was Mr. Harman, the man who was going to save me. Every day in Science, I'd picture it: how I'd show up one night on his doorstep, him opening the door, and how I wouldn't even have to say anything. How he'd see it all on my face like a bruise. Jesus, kid, he'd say.

But then he got fired for IM chats he had with an eighth-grade girl and it was like being doubly betrayed.

Now it's eighth grade: no Mr. Harman, no Maggie. She's not allowed to speak to me—not since her father caught me in the waterbed. *Sinful*, he said. I walk past our old table in the cafeteria just in case, but she doesn't look up. For a second, the other girls turn: ponytails smooth and shining, faces blank as daylight. I keep walking till I get to the very farthest table.

A girl named Melyssa with a Y touches her spiky necklace and says aren't I that girl Maggie's friend?

I look back at Maggie across the cafeteria. No, I say.

This one time, says Melyssa with a Y, I said God damnit in the hall and she was like, Damnit is *not* the Lord's last name.

Oh, I say. Weird.

Melyssa with a Y says she likes my jacket, which is Billy's old one from the Army. I found it in a box in the basement, and when he saw me wearing it, he said, Huh, look at that. He said better me wearing it than him.

Melyssa with a Y tells me to come with her to the gas station after school. That's where I meet him. That's where I meet Connor.

Connor's from our town, he says, but I've never seen him before. More than that, though, he doesn't seem like he's from anywhere. Like he just slipped through some rip in the universe. He's tall with green cauldron eyes, and when he leans in toward me behind the gas station, somehow I know it's him: the one who'll save me.

Mom and Billy hate him right away. He's seventeen, they say. He has a record, they say.

Connor stirs up something inside them. Billy slams the phone down when he calls. For two weeks straight, Mom barely drinks. She stays up late, guards the front door.

I know what you're doing, she says when I get too near.

But I can always outlast her because suddenly I don't need to sleep. All the time, I seem to be hovering someplace just off the ground.

Eskimo looks at me and won't stop looking. Like suddenly I'm the alien getting called off to space.

One night, I sneak Connor into my bed. He's been outside, in the trees. He smells like cigarettes and rain. He has a pale moon face that pulls. A face you can never quite see.

He says he failed his probation. He says, Let's run away.

Where? I say.

Anywhere.

The next night, I touch every object in my room, trying to find one important enough to bring. I look at my shelf lined with little objects: rocks and trinkets and souvenirs. They must have been collected by some other girl, someone I used to be. I shove the shoebox with all my CDs under Eskimo's car bed.

We'll keep going, I think. We'll keep going till we hit the ocean. We'll never once look back.

But instead we stop at an old house, windows punched in like black eyes. Inside, people scrawled on mattresses. Phone numbers sprawled on walls. No, I think. Other way around. *Sprawl, scrawl,* I say to myself as we climb up the stairs.

The attic is garbage and debris piled up to my knees. A stained and dirty mattress floating above. It looks like a raft drifting out to sea. For a second, I look out, dizzy, from the top of the stairs and think: *the ocean.* All this time I've been going toward it.

Connor sells some pills he stole. Bills change hands. Other things. Cigarette ash makes a ring around the mattress. On the ceiling, more phone numbers, none of them mine. (What if I forget my own phone number?) On the ceiling, one lone playing card. A jack of spades. I try to picture the person who must've pasted it there.

For a while, I want to leave and then I don't anymore. Time turns to water—nights, days—and I wonder if I could leave, if I'm even an *I* anymore. I'm in the walls like a smell. When police cars show up, people run. But gravity's gotten huge and strange and I think I could never leave this place even if I wanted to.

I'll hide here, I tell Connor. I'll hide in the walls.

Connor looks away, and I know then that he's gotten tired of me. He says they have police dogs. He says he could go to jail. Do I want that?

No.

He goes outside and I think maybe he's turning himself in, but instead he brings two policemen up to find me.

That true what he told us? they ask, and for a second I'm surprised they can see me—that I'm real and visible. You can't go home?

I nod.

The policemen look at each other and sigh. All right, they say in tired voices. Let's go.

Outside, I see I've missed it: the first snow. Night air cuts into me, smooth and clean. The street glows bright as bone. Then I'm in the back of a police car watching lights go red, blue, red on the snow.

Can he come? I ask about Connor. But the policemen don't talk to me. I wonder if I get a phone call.

At the police station, they leave me in a room full of filing cabinets and bright lights. I wonder how the world can go from dark to lights just like that.

A long while passes, and I wonder if the policemen forgot about me. There's a phone just sitting on a desk, and I don't know what else to do, so I call Maggie, who has her own phone line.

Hello? She sounds like she's been asleep, and suddenly I realize it's very late.

Hi, I say.

Where *are* you? she says. Everyone's really worried.

I tell her I'm at the police station, in a room full of filing cabinets.

Are you going to jail?

I don't know.

She tells me I should pray. That I should say the sinner's prayer. She's about to recite the words when I hear the policemen outside in the hall.

The father is here, one says to the other.

Then I see him: my father, who must've driven hours to come get me. I haven't seen him in a long time and I think I'm supposed to feel something now that he's here. But I feel nothing. He looks like a stranger.

Let's go, the stranger says.

My father is a stranger and his wife looks like Neil Diamond. Their house is quiet all the time. Sometimes I think it's like space and talking is actually impossible. Like you could scream and scream and no one would ever hear.

For the first two weeks, I miss Connor. Then some other feeling slides around inside me, slick and queasy. I go into the bathroom and cut off all my hair.

I talk to no one at my new school. My father asks about friends. Have I made any yet?

Sure, I nod.

Neil Diamond takes me shopping for clothes, and I hate them all. She buys a pack of glow-in-the-dark stars for my ceiling.

Don't you want to decorate your room? she asks.

I don't tell her this isn't my room, isn't my life. And if by some trick of the universe it *is* my life, then no way will I decorate it with glow-in-the-dark stars.

I walk to school and then back again. I stare and stare at my face in the mirror. Everywhere I go, it feels like sleepwalking. Like the whole world's on mute.

Sometimes at night, I hear tiny footsteps on the floorboards. They tiptoe across the room, then climb into my bed: a small round ghost curled into my spine. They can do this, ghosts. You just can't look back and see if they're really there.

On my birthday, I don't talk to anyone. I leave the house before my father gets up so he can't say happy birthday. Because my birthday means almost a year has passed since I came here, which is impossible.

After school, I walk around the empty house feeling cold. They keep it about zero degrees to save money. The phone rings and at first I think I won't pick up. But then I think, what if someone's dying or dead? So I answer.

Mom's voice is far and wavery. It's you, she says. Happy birthday, she says.

And then her voice hooks something inside me, and it comes up in shuddery animal sobs.

It'll be okay, says Mom, except now she's crying too. And anyway, I don't think she really means it, because we both know nothing can ever be okay.

But I don't say that. Instead I say how it's cold here all the time. How it's cold and silent like space. I hate it here, I say. I hate this house. I hate Neil Diamond.

Oh Laney, what did she *do?*

Nothing. I just hate everything *about* her.

Then Mom has to go. She promises to call again tomorrow.

From far away, a dial tone hums in my ear, and I make a list of all the things I know. Your name is Lane, I tell myself. You have brown hair, brown eyes. You like lists. You're fourteen.

There's a final meeting with my parents and Nancy, the caseworker who came once to my father's house and talked to me very slowly, like I couldn't understand. Case closure, this meeting's called, like a book shutting me forever inside it. Mom told me on the phone—we talk now every day after school in secret.

The morning before the meeting, my father gives me a ride to school. I'm late due to staying up all night debating the thing I'm about to do. And still I don't know. My hands shake. My heart clatters around like an empty bottle inside my chest.

But when we pull up to the school doors, my father talks before I can. He wants to ask, he says. Do I know anything about all the long-distance charges on the phone bill?

Too quick, I say no. Then: I don't know, maybe. Then I hand him the envelope. Inside's a letter that says I take it all back. Everything I said last year. Nothing happened at Mom's house. We never left, scared, in the middle of the night.

For Nancy, the envelope says.

For a second, my father just stares, like if he refuses to take it, he can stop the thing that's coming. Finally he says, I don't like surprises, Lane.

I mumble something and eject myself from the front seat, my head buzzing so loud I'm deaf for homeroom and the next three periods. All day, I picture Nancy reading my words aloud in her dumb, slow voice. Words can do things, it occurs to me. Not just say but do.

After school, I call Mom. I tell her I want to come home. Can I come home now?

There's a long pause. She says it's not that easy. She says she doesn't know.

Then I wait around for my father to get home from work. He must hate me now, I think.

But he doesn't seem to hate me. He doesn't say anything, really, till a few days later, when I'm late again and he's driving me to school. His voice gets weird and serious, and he says sometimes people recant things. Do I know what recant means?

No.

It means take something back, he says. Sometimes kids miss their families and take back the things they said. But that doesn't mean the things they said aren't true.

I want to tell him that I'm not one of those kids, but suddenly talking has become impossible. A tiny me keeps getting smaller and smaller inside my chest. I think I was a liar when I said nothing, a liar when I said something, and a liar now that I've recanted the thing I said. No one will ever understand this.

Two weeks later, we're at ZooAmerica. Mom, Billy, Eskimo, and me. Me, who always hated the zoo, hated seeing the trapped animals in their cages. Suddenly I never want to leave. I watch us from someplace up above: Eskimo signing at the penguins, Billy consulting the map, Mom pushing strands of hair out of my eyes. I freeze-frame us in the watery light. My family.

Because here is how the day will go: this family, us, we'll walk around every corner of the zoo. We'll go next door, to Funtown, and get flung around on the bumper cars. *Again*, Eskimo will sign. *Again*. Stuffed animal prizes will fall down into our hands. Cotton candy will stick in our hair. Then it'll come time to pile into the car and drive home.

I'm not going with them.

And the crazy way the sun is hitting everything right now, the thought of them going home—the thought of them going home *without* me—lifts me up and out of my skin. Like by some trick of the crazy light, I've become a kind of floating, queasy and unreal.

I want to come too, I tell Mom in the parking lot, my voice rising high like a little kid's. Not just for dinner but to sleep *over*. I want to carry Eskimo on my back up the stairs. I want to fall asleep in my real bed, in the bedroom Mom and Billy painted blue.

You'll have to ask your father, Mom says.

Which means no.

Still, I do it. I go to the payphone and dial the numbers just to defer the hard thud of knowing. The way it pulls the floor out from my chest, drops me into awful certainty: here is my family, and they are powerless to save me.

My father is quiet for a minute. Then finally he says, I don't think that's such a good idea, Lane.

He says we should take things slow. He says maybe in a month.

What will be different in a month? I want to ask but recant it. A month is a whole eternity and I've already waited even longer than that. I turn to look at Mom and Billy and Eskimo all standing by the car, their faces far and quavery, a highway mirage that keeps moving out of reach.

I look at them and a part of me would like to wrench my heart free. But I know that really will be the end then: my heart will be gone, nothing, a black and bloodied pulp.

And I think the way I've thought many times this year: I've done something for which there's no undoing. Only it was easier before, alone. Now I can see, just on the other side of the payphone glass, How Things Used to Be. And even if How Things Used to Be is cloudy and uncertain, possibly unreal, I know there was at least one true moment and my whole life depends on getting back to it.

So here I am, a liar and a recanter, hanging up the payphone at the zoo. I turn back toward the car, already knowing what I have to do.

It's seventh period when I walk out of school. This is how it feels, I tell myself. This is how it feels to walk out of school, out of town. This is how it feels to walk out of your own life.

I take the local bus into the city and get lost trying to find the Greyhound station. I've written down the address on a slip of paper, but instead of a bus station there's only a man shouting numbers beneath a bodega lottery sign. For a second, I wonder if this man is somehow, impossibly, the bus station—if he calls down the buses from thin air.

The days are short now and already the light is slanted and slipping. I decide to retrace my footsteps and start all over again. But soon as I turn, I see it: dark glass and buses gliding in and out. Even numbers, I remember, go on the other side of the street.

At the ticket counter, I have to count out the last few dollars in quarters while the ticket man watches. I've saved my lunch money all year, not knowing why, but now I see I was saving it for this moment.

I have a story all planned out. I'm going to visit my aunt, I'll say. I'm going to visit my aunt on the other side of the country.

But the ticket man doesn't ask. He just looks at me and says, You done this before?

I nod.

In the sweaty underbelly of the bus station, people stand in lines, mumbling. Buses hiss and sigh in the dark. I watch them light up and take off like ghost ships into the night.

When they call out my bus, I squeeze in next to a window in the back. A wheezing man falls asleep next to me, his head rolling like something detached onto my shoulder.

But once we're going, nothing matters. When you're going, you're no place—you're in between. Through the smudged bus window, I watch the world float by: the neon lights of gas stations, cars stunned and frozen in a state of wonder. Something unseeable at the corner of my eye. Far away, the horizon pulls like floodwaters.

For the first two days, I'm afraid to fall asleep. The wheezing man gets off after only a few stops, and then I put my backpack on the seat next to me. Sometimes I lie down and close my eyes, but always I stay awake to keep watch from between my eyelashes.

Nobody interrogates me like I expected. Nobody asks why I'm alone. A lady with a bird's face offers me Fig Newtons out of a Ziploc bag. An old man gnarled as a fist drops penciled drawings into my lap: sunflowers, a bunch of daisies. *May flowers make you happy*, he writes underneath.

Then one night I do fall asleep. It feels like just a second, but when I wake up, light is coming through the bus windows and one of my earrings is gone. Not just any earring but one of the tiny gold hoops I was wearing the day I left Mom's, a year ago.

All the clothes I was wearing that day have become important. Like the Army jacket, which I've barely taken off all year. Sometimes I think it's like ghosts, the way they have to keep wearing the clothes they died in.

It's true that I've become sort of obsessed with dead things. I found *The Tibetan Book of the Dead* on my father's bookshelf, and even though it made no sense, I kept reading. *One such as you will awaken as if from sleep.*

That's a little morbid, isn't it? said Neil Diamond.

No, I scowled.

Because really, it's not death, even, the thing I keep trying to understand. More like, I can't tell what it means to be alive anymore. And now that the earring's gone, there's some part of me I'll never get back.

This bus ride was supposed to cure me. I was supposed to figure everything out. Now I look out at the rows of frozen cornfields and wonder if this is just how it is, if you just keep losing parts of yourself forever wherever you go.

We transfer buses in the dark and I get stuck right behind the driver, who talks to me nonstop. He says he's driven this road so many times he can drive with his eyes closed, he can drive it asleep. He says the road's like his own palm line, and all he has to do is blink to see.

Darkness rises up off the ground, and the sun's a far fire coming through the trees. Up ahead I see something white and glimmering on a truck top. My heart flutters up to my throat: snow. But then I see it's not snow, just the truck's white roof catching the light.

The bus rolls and keeps rolling. Like a wheel that can't ever stop. Signs say: THE END IS NEAR. Say: BUCKLE UP. Say: GIRLS, GIRLS, GIRLS.

Two guys who look like mountain men talk to me at the next stop. They ask how old I am.

Seventeen, I say.

When I tell them I'm going all the way to the ocean, to California, they say seventeen is awful young to be going cross-country. I say I'm going to visit my aunt.

Later, they stop and say goodbye. Can't sleep on that bus no more, they say. Be careful in California, they say.

The bus starts up again, merging onto the highway. My fingers *tap-tap* on the windowpane, and for the first time I feel afraid. I hadn't thought about what I'd do once I got to California. I hadn't thought about coming to a stop.

From a mountaintop, by helicopter.

From zombies, by vaccine.

Ghost ship, Morse code.

Lost at sea.

Then just like that, night comes and the alien-ghost is sitting right next to me. I stay very still. If I move, he might turn out to be nothing, a trick of light, and then I'll be alone again. So instead I stare straight ahead while around me bodies mutter and sigh, shift in their sleep. In the dark, you can hear how close we all are. How close and how far.

House, the alien-ghost signs. Ghosts always want something from you. *Look at me*, they say. *Build me a house.*

But I can't—not right now. *I have to keep going*, I say. Whatever ship this is, whatever dark I'm sailing through, there's no telling the way back. Not even if I knew all the stars, all the planets. Not even if I had every lost earring.

Except I don't know how to say all that, and anyway, the alien-ghost is looking someplace else. His fingers are short and stubby, drawing lines in the window fog. At first, I think he's writing his answer, but instead he points out the window: *Look.*

All at once, I see it. Through the fog: a trickle, a leak. Dark sky and fields, bright hole of moon. How it comes at you in gasps and pieces, the world telling and telling. Something fast and rushing. Something too quick for words.

I turn around fast, my heart skipping like a stone. But there's no one there. The seat next to me is empty.

The bus stops outside Cheyenne, flat as forever, and all of a sudden, I wonder if I'm far enough. I wonder if I'm far enough to go back.

And I think I hadn't fully known till right this minute: I hadn't known I was coming back.

From inside the phone booth, I look out: the parking lot smudged with winter light, the sky godless and huge. I remember how I was supposed to know it all by now, what happened and why. But however you say it, it's just words, and they're never the right ones. They're always a lie or a prayer.

A pulse *tap-taps* in my ear like a code. Enter into my heart, you're supposed to say. That's the prayer. But how can you ever even know your heart—what's in it or why?

And I think that right now I'm so close. Like if I squint, I can see it just beyond the glass of the phone booth, a highway mirage that keeps moving out of reach. *Home.*

So here I am, a liar and a recanter and now a runaway too, dialing the numbers home. Where are you? they'll ask. Where in God's name *are* you?

Because in truth, I know all the words already. I know all the words I'll say and all the words they'll say. How they'll say, Yes, of course, come home. Everything forgiven, every last thing.

But even as I dial the numbers one by one, something is stopping me. Some thud of knowing I must defer. A weariness comes over me like I'm a thousand years old.

This is what you wanted all this time, I tell myself. To be spirited from where you are. To be saved from something too big to know.

Just *call.*

But all of a sudden I can't. I just can't. Slowly I put down the phone.

1-800-FAT-GIRL

This was the summer they entered phone booths and ran out shrieking. They were ten, flat-chested in bathing suits. Secrets smooth as sea glass. Limbs wrung like seaweed. They crowded into payphones, sweat-sticky and iridescent with sunscreen.

No one could say where the number came from. It seemed to them that one day it just appeared—a line thrown across some unfathomable breach.

You've reached 1-800-FAT-GIRL. We've got plenty of girls to go all the way around. So pull it out and stick it in. Your credit card, that is.

Each time it was the same: they ran from the phone booth shrieking, gasping from laughter.

The fat girl's voice was watery and strange. The oldest heard an echo. The youngest, a ghost. The quietest said it was like a seashell, the ocean rolling in your ear.

Where did the fat girls live? *A basement*, someone said. *A cave.*

Maybe in a cave made *of fat.*

How could a cave be made of fat?

It would be all gloopy. Like one big waterbed.

The fat girls slept on waterbeds—this was the one thing on which they all agreed.

●

Days, they tanned in front yards. They draped themselves across towels, eyes low and watchful, darting like bees.

They tanned. They chanted. They stole the baseball caps of boys. They were shameless. They were bored.

What do the fat girls do if nobody calls?

They just sit around. Eat jelly from the jar.

Time's different there. It doesn't move except when someone calls.

At night, the fat girl's voice followed them. It hummed nothing songs. Sat around leafing through their older sisters' magazines. When their parents fought, it snuck outside, kept them company on the swings. Even in the dark, you knew it was always there—an ocean rolling toward infinity.

They watched. They whispered. They grew their secrets like pearls. At night, they dreamt their houses were on fire. Dream air pinned them down.

Their secrets changed, then changed again. They parsed the world for hidden clues: song lyrics, radio ads, the passing comments of neighbors. *She'll be a looker when she grows up.*

They looked. They whispered. They threw themselves at each other's older brothers. At night, they burned up in secret flames.

Years passed. Their fathers blushed and turned away. Their mothers lay passed out on the couch. Their older sisters became black holes, perpetual disappearances in the night.

They still threw themselves at each other's older brothers, but only when no one was looking, only in the dark. They became ascetics, eating nothing. They became ravenous, eating everything. They didn't remember the fat girl. Their eyes lost their sting.

●

It was the youngest who heard it again, one night wandering sleepless through her house. She'd woken from a dream of eating everything inside the refrigerator, and she moved through the dark hall, panicked, to see if it was true. When she saw that it wasn't, she stood still for a minute, transfixed by the glow of the open door as though waiting for a sign.

At school the next day, the others stared at her blankly.

Heard what? they asked.

The voice. The fat girl.

They shook their heads.

Remember? The payphone?

They blushed and turned away. It was like stumbling upon evidence of a self they'd long since disavowed. They didn't like to be reminded.

But that night, the voice pricked them each awake. When they finally drifted uneasily into sleep, it dripped like a leaky faucet through their dreams.

They endured the school day, then assembled wordlessly in the hall. They looked at each other and gave slow nods.

That night, in the phone booth, it was the youngest who dialed, squinting at the numbers on her mother's credit card. The others held their breath, leaned in close.

Yeah? The voice sounded tired, like they'd disturbed her from sleep.

Hi, said the oldest, louder than she meant to.

A pause.

You girls, the fat girl said finally. *You used to call and run away shrieking.*

They blushed in the dark. *So what if it was us?*

So nothing. I liked you better then, is all. I got to sit around all day on the waterbed, eat jelly from the jar. Now it's a new operator, new rules. The fat girl sighed like they couldn't understand.

So what do you do now?

That's the problem: it's like floating around a black hole. Or like being one. Everything goes into you and nothing sticks. A story running backward till you're nothing at all.

When they called again the next night and the next, the fat girl laughed. *Knew you'd be back*, she said.

They became insomniacs, sliding around all directions of the night. Everywhere they went, the fat girl's voice followed, sweet and terrible as a lullaby.

Tell us more about how it used to be.

Used to be when?

When we used to call.

Well, there was a cave, for one thing. And I could hear the ocean, for another. Doesn't that sound lovely?

Yes, they agreed. *Lovely.*

And I had a whole necklace full of pearls. Each one used to sing to me in the night.

At school, they never spoke of the fat girl. Days were hard and full of edges. At night, they became formless, fleshless. The dark opened like a valve.

Sometimes the voice dared them: *You could burn this house down*, it said. *You could.*

The nights grew wide, and they wandered, sleepless. They swallowed pills, lied about their ages. Climbed in and out of the backs of cars. They watched from someplace outside their bodies as dream air pinned them down. Sometimes they had the feeling this was a story they'd heard already, that the fat girl had always been there, narrating in their ears.

A story moving backward. In which case, the fathers they remembered would soon return. Their mothers would startle awake. Their sisters would emerge from the backs of cars, unvanished from the dark. The nights would grow smaller and opaque with sleep—tiny as pearls, closing back inside the heart.

They themselves would grow younger. They'd grow sure and true—limbs wrung like seaweed, secrets smooth as sea glass. It would be like running toward the ocean at night: you couldn't see it, but you knew it was there. Relics and sea life beneath the waves.

Or they'd emerge: fleshless, formless, their hearts flung open. Pearls everywhere, spangled like stars.

COMING TO

1. *vein*

From Old French *veine*, from Latin *vena*. The earliest senses were *blood vessel* and *small natural underground channel of water*. See also: *blood, artery, channel, the channeling of the dead*.

It's a wake, we are told, my cousin and I, but we hear it like one word: awake. Who is doing the waking? We don't ask. We are six. We know there's a body and the body is her father. But *how* the body is her father is harder to say. He's become a dark spot hovering just above our eyelids, a presence that tilts the whole room. We move through it like we would a funhouse, not knowing what's real—everything swollen and overwrought, red velour everywhere and grown-ups stiff as wax. They whisper out of the sides of their mouths like bad renditions of ghosts. Beneath them, we cling to each other—hands, wrists, fingernails—and we move this way, like one four-legged creature, up the narrow carpet toward the coffin.

A small stool sits beside it, waiting. We look at each other and know what we must do. She whispers, as if to prepare me: *They drain all the blood out when you die.*

•

We are bowed heads in the dark, wakeful at 1 a.m. We are shapeless. We are voices, saying and unsaying.

She tells me again about the man who fell on a nail and punctured his wrist. This is the year she's interested in death.

So what happened?

Her so-what shrug. *He died. He spilled out through his veins.*

This is the year we are eight. The year we become creatures with blood, veins: spillable things. I start looking away from my own wrist, fragile now as a bird's neck and equally fraught. Blue-gray veins run through it like thin wicks of flame. Veins are terrifying; veins are bewitching, a ghostly glimpse of some bad end. Veins are inside you, which means there's no escape.

The first time it happens, there's no blood, no veins. I'm sixteen and sitting in a doctor's office. The nurse squeezes her blood pressure pump and sighs. *Can't get a pulse on you.*

Maybe you don't have a pulse, suggests my mother. *Maybe you're dead.*

I don't know yet what to expect. Later, it will start to prick faint and familiar—the way gravity loosens and churns, the way the back of my head becomes a queasy universe, unfathomably deep. But that first time—the time I faint on the word *dead*—I wash straight into nothing.

Fainting undoes the world and remakes it. It seeps: once it begins, it won't stop. It becomes its own logic, a mythology slowly coalescing. I faint in doctor's offices, in bathrooms. I faint at the mention of blood, hearts, veins. I faint at mentions of sex, alien probes, enemas. I faint at the word *epidural*, having confused it with *enema*. I faint trying to use a tampon. I faint at the sight of three drops of blood on tile. I faint at the thought of fainting. My own heartbeat unnerves me.

2. *faint*

Middle English: *cowardly* surviving in the phrase *faint heart*; from Old French *faint*, related to *feign*, stem of *feindre*: to make a pretense of a feeling or response, invent a story or allegation. From Latin *fingere*: to mold, contrive, make.

I've been in Phnom Penh a month when the faintings begin. They come across my desk in a brief: sixty workers fainting in a garment factory. They faint not one by one but all together—fainting at the sight of fainting. Like most garment workers, they are women, nearly all of them very young.

More mass faintings follow at other garment factories: sixty, seventy, a hundred women at a time. The women speak of dizziness, of ghosts. Sometimes these are the same thing. *There was darkness all over my face.*

I'm twenty-five, working at a newspaper, and mostly my own bouts of fainting have come and gone. But now, sitting in the paper's cramped offices, I start to think about fainting again—what it says and what it unsays. The way the fainter turns from the world even as her body points mutely back. Because what is more submissive than fainting, what more yielding than the swoon? And yet, how quicker to call attention to the body than when one—or many—falls suddenly to the floor?

Factory owners accuse the women of feigning. Chemical experts and engineers draw up reports. Healers are called. Monks perform elaborate ceremonies. And still the women keep fainting.

Faint heart, we say of someone who is timid or afraid. Oum, my Khmer teacher, tells me there's a similar phrase in Khmer: *khsaoy beh daung*. Weak heart—often used to describe one who faints.

Oum and I sit quietly at his kitchen table, going page by page through my Khmer book. But sometimes, out of nowhere, a word will come and all but carry Oum off, and when this happens, he has to stand and gesture. What he likes best is tracing the labyrinthine paths of words through history—across eras and wars and invasions, from Sanskrit and Pali up through mistranslations by the French. He does this in a way that's at once transfixing and impossible to follow. I understand all the pieces, but never how they fit together.

The word for wind is *khyâl*—said to move through the body at all times, much like blood. Some say the dizziness that presages fainting arises from a rush of wind and blood to the head. *Khyâl goeu*, this is called. Wind attack.

But dizziness, Oum tells me, is also a common way of speaking about distress. *He shakes me,* one might say. *He makes my soul dizzy.*

3. *dizzy*

Old English *dysig*: foolish; related to Low German *dusig, dösig*: giddy. Perhaps from *dheu*: dust, vapor, smoke; to rise in a cloud (and related notions of defective perception or wits). Having a whirling sensation, empty-headed, shaking, weak. Used of the *foolish virgins* in early translations of Matthew.

We stand atop the stool and watch him inside his coffin. The surprising thing isn't that he's dead or stiff or even drained. What surprises me most is that he's actual and there—that he takes up space in the same world we do, a pillow dented beneath his head.

And then the stool begins to shake. It happens slow and also fast—the stool teetering beneath us, our knees giving way. The satin of the coffin is red and gleaming, and I know: *That's where I'm going.*

No one can save me from it. No grown-up, no God. Not even my cousin beside me.

But when I open my eyes, we're not inside the coffin. Instead, we're tangled together between coffin and stool, grown-ups coming to fish us out. The aftershock of falling drags little animal cries from our throats, and it startles me, this sound—the sound of the world flooding back, voices washing over us. A moment before, I was alone, teetering at the brink of nothingness. An aloneness creeps its tendrils up my spine.

At the cemetery, we play freeze tag. We know to run fast. We know which grave to avoid. Winter light sets the stones ablaze, and they flash at us like gleaming cauldrons in the ground. But we run so quick, nothing can stick to us—not a mumbled hymn in the distance, not even his name. When we get too close, my cousin turns her face away.

We never speak of him, though sometimes, sitting in the back of her mother's car, my cousin starts writhing and shrieking beside me. *I forget!* she screams. *I forget!*

She means his face. This is the first disappearance. Her mother starts carrying a picture of him everywhere so she can see.

Sitting beside her in the back of the car, I start to think of ghosts as faceless, just chapped flaps of skin where their faces would be. It pains them, I think, in an odd transposition—not her pain, but theirs.

At night, we tell ghost stories in my basement, though how the ghosts are in them is sometimes hard to say. The rusty nail could be the ghost. The veins.

My cousin's voice is always coming untethered, rising up and up toward the cellar beams. *Be quiet,* I'm always whispering. *Be quiet.* Upstairs, there are footsteps, voices jagged and sudden—staticky ghosts in some wrong frequency. I'm always more afraid.

One night, she has a story about a drunk who throws his children out a second-story window. In this story, I think, the window is the ghost. Or maybe the falling.

I know what she's waiting for. I know what she's asking: *What ghosts live in this house?* But I just turn my face away toward the dark. You can never call the ghosts by name.

4. *ghost*

Old English *gāst* (in the sense of spirit, soul), of Germanic origin: wrath, wraith, horrible, frightful. Connected to the idea of the wound: to rip, to tear, to pull to pieces, to find oneself undone. The voice that speaks through the wound.

The women come from villages in the countryside, and they bring their ghosts with them. They are fasteners; they are spinners. They sew on tags: Nike, Puma, Gap. Around them, machines click their silver clicks.

The women live in dormitory-style buildings—six, seven, eight to a room—waking before daylight and piling into trucks. At the factories, they're told not to speak. Bright blue surgical masks blot out their mouths.

When they first come to the factory, the women are spooked by the machines—their mechanical juts and stabs, the endless noise. They sit in lines, facing in one direction. Between the surgical masks that cover their mouths and the paper scarves that pull back their hair, only their eyes are visible.

Sometimes they go on strike. On my way to work, I see them chanting in the streets. Riot police shoot tear gas into the crowds as the women sing protest songs. *O! Ma! Ma! I can't tell night from day... Dizzy and fruitless, hoping one day for health, spinning, until the day we return to our beloved mothers.*

•

Oum tells me that night panic is called *khmaoch sângkât*: the ghost pushes you down. Dreams, he says, arise from the wanderings of the soul while the body sleeps. This is why, recounting a dream, one speaks in terms of the soul, never *I*. A dream of a particular place, for instance, means the soul has left the body to journey there in the night: *My soul went to a rice field in the countryside*. A ghost attack signals a soul in danger of becoming dislodged: *The ghost strangled my soul's neck*.

In our office, there's a woman whose father is rumored to have worked at Tuol Sleng, the torture and extermination center. But these are just whispers. Encoded silences. You don't talk about the things you know. *Don't take your heart out of your chest to let the bird peck it.*

Dara, the oldest reporter at the paper, was seven in 1975, the year of the fall. He lost his parents and all five siblings. I'm not sure how I know this, just that these things are known. Encoded. At story meetings, he frequently begins: *Yesterday at lunchtime, when I was at the brothel—*

It's hard to know which stories of the Pol Pot years are true. Their scarcity turns each into a kind of parable. I hear the story, for instance, of the woman who escaped the work camps and managed to make her way back to the city. But the city had been emptied; no one lived there anymore. She found her way to her old neighborhood, to her old street. She walked the empty sidewalks like someone returning from the dead, looking for something, anything, to remind her. But when she found her house, she knew she couldn't stay.

Not even ghosts lived there, she said.

•

One day, Dara comes and pulls a chair up beside me. *My life is like a bamboo train*, he says, apropos of nothing. *Many ups, many downs.*

He sees the Khmer homework sitting on my desk and points to the word *spin*.

The word spin is the same as overwhelmed, he tells me. *Your soul spins out of your body.*

5. spin

Old English *spinnan*: draw out and twist; related to *spinnen*: spinner, spider. To weave, plait, braid, spin yarns. See also: *the three Fates*, esp. Clotho—*she who spins.*

We put our ears to walls and knock, searching for secret passages. We hold séances and petition the dark: *Who are you? What is your name?* We run away screeching, not waiting for the reply. Sometimes you name a thing you don't want to name.

When my cousin goes home, the clocks tick still, and night lies close and heavy. I stay up late. I keep watch.

In the mornings, the world is mostly where I left it. There are things nameless and familiar as my own skin. They take up space and no space at all. The empty wineglass always on my bookshelf in the morning, a dot like dried blood at the center. The way my feet stick to the kitchen floor. Dried liquor from a thrown bottle. Broken glass like cracked bits of light.

But sometimes it's not the same world at all.

One morning when my cousin is visiting, I wake up and find I can't move my legs. They feel like they no longer belong to me, like they've forgotten how to work. I think for a minute that I'm a ghost, disappearing in reverse. It's the morning she's supposed to leave. Cat-astrophic things always seem to happen when she leaves.

I have to be carried out to the car and into the doctor's office, where I sit on crackly paper, afraid. But just before the doctor lays his hands on me, my legs shudder awake. Fear sets them running again.

There are ways to leave the world, though most require dying. It's true that you leave at night, asleep, but when you wake the next morning, the world is still mostly the one you expect. After fainting, the world you come back to isn't the one you left. It takes long minutes to become familiar again. Or it takes long minutes to believe: *Yes, this is the world—the real one, mine.*

Coming to, this is called. There are the usual questions: where and when. But before that, there's something else. Not who am I or even what, but a question of being an *I* at all.

If you're *coming to*, there must also then be the question of where you're coming from.

6. *tongue*

Old English: *tunge*, of Germanic origin; related to Dutch *tong* and Latin *lingua*: language, dead language, forgotten tongue. The thing that slips from the tip of the tongue.

Some of the women break into tongues before fainting. Afterward, they recall sensing an omen of blood running through the factory. They describe a dark path they can't see with their eyes.

At a Chinese-owned factory, one woman screams in Mandarin, demanding offerings to the local ancestral spirit, or *neak tā*. The woman is possessed by a ghost, some say. The factory owners have failed to make the proper offerings.

The women scream, bent over in pain. Their eyes roll back in their heads. But afterward, they can't remember what they've said.

•

I find myself reading about the possessed at Loudun, the site of one of Europe's largest mass possessions in the seventeenth century. They too were young women and girls in cramped quarters—a convent of Ursuline nuns. They spoke in a high Latin they claimed not to understand.

At the ensuing trials, which went on for years, the possessing demons liked to play tricks, refusing, for instance, to state their names. *Enemies of God*, they said, or they shrieked with hysterical laughter. *Ha-ha, did not tell you.*

I forgot my name, said one. *I can't find it.*

Another: *I lost it in the wash.*

7. *darkness*

Old English *deorc*, of Germanic origin, related to *tarnen*: conceal, hide, disappear. Dark smoke, dark shadows, the looming dark. *But darkness came.* A stab in the dark.

During the Khmer Rouge years, words weren't just words anymore. The Khmer nation, Oum says, was known as *machine*, from the French. The word *blood* became glittering and transcendent: *The sublime blood of the workers.* The year was known as Year Zero, as though time itself had stopped.

Asked about this term decades later, Nuon Chea—Brother Number Two, as he is better known—says that poverty was zeroed, corruption was zeroed. *Many things were zeroed.*

The enemy had to be smashed, he says. The Khmer Rouge had a policy of *smashing*—used metaphorically to refer to the struggle against perceived enemies but also as a euphemism for killing. Victims were sent by the truckload to mass graves. They were pushed to their knees and clubbed in the back of the head so that they fell forward, zeroed, into the ground. Some trucks were filled entirely with children. In official records, they're noted only as *smashed*.

A prison without walls, some call those years. *Fire without smoke.*

The regime was known only as Angkar—roughly translating to *the organization*, though it took on a kind of all-seeing impermeability, a force at once ungraspable and close. Often it was described as having the eyes of a pineapple, a panopticon seeing in all directions.

Angkar was vast, godlike and all-knowing, yet it was also intimate and near. It forced marriages between strangers upon threat of rape or execution. It dragged its victims off in the middle of the night. Soldiers sometimes appeared in doorways to say that Angkar had asked for a family's son. This was how a word wasn't the same word anymore, Oum says. *To ask* came to mean *to take away and kill.*

8. *body*
   Of unknown origin.

Who are you? we ask the dark. *What is your name?*
   We run away before we get to the last question.
   How did you die?

At fifteen, we starve ourselves or we run away from home. We are possessed. We are stricken with things we can't say. Our own names sound strange to us. Our eyes roll back in our heads.

This is the year we are trapped: inside houses, inside rooms. The body itself. We are held captive in our skin.

By sixteen, we begin to believe our mothers. *Maybe you don't have a pulse. Maybe you're dead.* They've merely spoken aloud what we secretly believe—that we've already begun to disappear.

I forgot my name. I can't find it.
I lost it in the wash.

One witness to the Loudun trials recounted: *And when she was brought to say, "My God, take possession of my soul and my body," the devil twice took her by the throat when she tried to say "my body," causing her to shout, grind her teeth, and stick out her tongue. Forced at last to obey, she received the holy sacrament that the spirit had several times attempted to make come out of her mouth by causing her to vomit.... It took more than half an hour to receive it, she being so agitated that six to seven people could not restrain her. She could not worship God; but finally she opened her mouth afterward and communed peacefully.*

9. *tongue*

Old English: *tunge*, of Germanic origin; related to Dutch *tong* and Latin *lingua*. To find one's tongue, speak. To lose one's tongue, go mute.

Rape-murder is not a real word, but we use it anyway. The copy chief debates the term but is overruled. Almost every day, there's at least one rape in the paper. They are child rapes or gang rapes or both. Sometimes they are rape-murders. We make jokes about these stories and judge newcomers by their response. The ones who protest, we know, will not work out.

From the start, I know to keep quiet. For the first few months, I have to wait while the panicky animal in my chest subsides, but then I feel nothing. Or I feel nothing until one day I'm rewriting notes from a Cambodian reporter. The story is about the rape of a sixteen-year-old who, having discovered she was pregnant, tried to kill herself by drinking shampoo. But suddenly, as I type, the words no longer look like words—they've become ants marching off the screen. Gravity comes loose.

In the office, we're always pressed for space, and the copy chief sits so close to me that our elbows touch. I can feel him reading over my shoulder. He intones: *Unfortunately, the shampoo was Johnson & Johnson's No More Tears.* I start to laugh and then can't stop laughing. The possessed at Loudun also sometimes could not stop laughing. For a second I fear I'll never be able to stop.

There are ways to leave the body, but few of them are quick. Even dying takes time. Fainting is brief extinction—spasm or swoon. Fainting comes and is gone.

But what is it that leaves the body? And what is it, then, that *comes to?*

Sometimes it appears to me like a silent movie—darkness and then a grainy film flickering before my eyes, a cast of unknown characters. But who is doing the watching? In these moments, there's no one looking out from behind my eyes, no watcher—just the reeling nothingness of space. The mind spins like a wheel.

10. *darkness*

Old English *deorc*: to fall dark, to be in the dark; unknown, unknowing. The dark that uncovers the dark.

I'm on the back of Dara's motorbike when he tells me: *I fainted once in the work camp.* We're headed toward the hospital, where a group of fainting women have been taken.

It was common to faint, he goes on. A response to overwork and starvation, to the sight of dead and decaying bodies. He calls it *khsaoy beh daung*: weak heart. *Many people died of weak hearts.*

At the hospital, the fainting women are crowded into small rooms, attached to IV drips. They sip juice boxes, and mostly they don't answer my questions. *What did it feel like? What do you remember?*

They turn to Dara and say something I can't understand. He smiles. *They say your voice is very quiet.*

One day, the managing editor asks Dara a question about one of his stories, and Dara becomes so incensed his face slides away. Rage appears to float him up and out of his body, and he shouts at the managing editor, *I'll kill you. I'll kill your whole family.* Afterward, he looks around, his hand pressed against his heart, as though he can't quite say who he is or where.

11. *ghost*

Old English *gāst* (in the sense of spirit, soul): noisy ghost, quiet ghost, wakeful ghost. Vengeful, blundering, lonely ghost. The thing that moves too quick for words. *Who walks among us like a ghost.*

At sixteen, I return again from running away—I can't seem to stop. Running away is a kind of fit, a spasm. It shoots me out, this last time, on the other side of the country. But afterward, it's impossible to speak about.

My cousin and I regard each other warily. My tongue has gone slow and heavy, and anyway, she looks like a stranger. *Who are you?* I want to ask. *What is your name?* Our faces hang hollow. Whatever language once existed between us is gone.

Who are you? What is your name?

And the question we could never quite manage: *How did you die?*

I wander through a twelfth-century temple, huge and dark and cool. A young girl dashes in and out of the shadows, grinning back at me. It becomes a game; I pretend not to see her, and she runs farther, every so often peeking back and giggling, winding deeper and deeper through the stone halls. She stops short at a small glowing shrine.

A temple laywoman looks up at us and motions for my hand. She knots a red string around my wrist and whispers a prayer I don't understand. For no reason at all, I burst into tears.

The next week, Oum points to the string around my wrist and teaches me the words for *weak* and *light in the body*. The woman who tied the string, he says, was refastening my soul to my skin.

12. *dizzy*

Old English *dysig*: foolish; related to Low German *dusig, dösig*: whirling, lightheaded, stupefied, stupor, stunned. Struck senseless, struck asunder.

The year I'm twenty, I live in Banaras, India. One night, at a dinner at my Hindi professor's house, there's some talk of blood and I can feel the world giving way. When I open my eyes, two wizened old ladies peer down at me through thin, translucent veils. They're the house's cooks, I realize later, but for what feels like hours, I look at them and don't know who or what I am. Something inside me has come dislodged. I can't remember my own name.

In Banaras, I'm writing my senior thesis on spirit possession. Every day, I take a rickshaw across the city to the tomb of a Sufi saint, a *mazar*, where women come to rid themselves of ghosts. At the time, I see no connection between possession and fainting. What I'm interested in is the interchange between shared and private symbols— whatever that means. I explain it to people as the reason there are no alien abductions in rural India and very few spirit possessions in the United States.

Fainting is something I have few words for, whereas I have many words for spirit possession. The women unbraid their hair (ghosts hide in braids) and flail their bodies, sometimes spinning in circles.

Voices tumble from their throats raw and deep, and family members crouch around them to ask: *Who are you? What do you want?* But afterward, the women can say little about these voices. They re-braid their hair and smile demurely. *I forget*, they say.

One day at the *mazar*, I hear a word that surprises me. *Khailna*: to play. At first I think I've misunderstood, but then I hear it again. I keep hearing it—women describing their trance states as play. *Khailna* can mean many things. A child's play or the playing of an instrument; to play a part, to perform.

Fainting, of course, has its own performative etymology, related to *feint* and *feign*. To make something, it implies. To create—to say. But what is it that fainting says? What blow does it feint? The answers never stick. It's like asking *What does the unsayable say?* We don't know—it only repeats. Its gaps unsay us.

13. *spin*

To stretch, to twist, to writhe. See: *Clotho, she who spins.* To turn rapidly, to come unturned. To spin yarns (stemming from *garnan, ghere*: intestines, guts; colloquially *stories*); to be witness to the story's entrails spun and unspun.

I've been in Phnom Penh a year when armed guards are called in at a factory strike in the city of Bavet. The strikers throw rocks at the windows of the factory, which manufactures shoes for Puma. Police are already assembled, riot shields at the ready, when a man enters through the factory gates and fires his gun into the crowd. A bullet enters the back of a twenty-one-year-old woman, piercing her lung and exiting through her chest. It lodges in the body of another woman, eighteen, standing nearby. A third woman is shot in the arm.

After the crowds disperse, the factory grounds are dotted with dark red shoeboxes.

A picture is released of the shooter, and he is quickly identified as the city governor. Government officials arrive at the hospital where the three women are recovering, one in critical condition. The officials offer money in exchange for silence, but the women refuse. They go on to give testimony at the trial a year later. Their wounds still cause them pain, they tell the court. Their bodies go weak, betray them. They are afraid every day.

After testifying, they return to work at the factory. The governor is never arrested.

14. *vein*

A blood vessel or small underground channel of water. To be the vessel that carries one across; to be the stream that runs alive, beneath.

Duel sanlap is how fainting is most often described in Khmer: falling and the loss of consciousness. But words are never that simple. *Sanlap* comes from *lap*, or loss, though it may also mean a fluid and whirling type of memory. Perhaps not coincidentally, the word is sometimes mispronounced *sralap*—darkness following a bright day.

In English, the terminology is no less muddy. For centuries, the medical term for fainting was lipothymia. *To leave the mind.* It differed from death, it was said, only in degree. Syncope, meanwhile, is a *cerebral eclipse*, though it can also mean an elision, a quickening of time. In music, it's a weak beat followed by a strong. It comes from the Greek roots for *sun* and *to cut*: it cuts off each time. It upends, escapes.

•

The greatest fear, I sometimes think, is that we are trapped: in bodies, in rooms, in time. Or the greatest fear is that we are not—that we can spill wide open.

If one is, as Kafka says, dead in one's own lifetime, then the heart thuds a traitorous song: *alive, alive.* These are the things that move unseen: blood, wind. The heart, which opens and closes invisibly, by what internal mechanism we can never really say.

Fainting, then, is catastrophe or exodus. It's an underworld that erupts in broad daylight. Fainting is a darkness, a flare.

In Khmer, Oum tells me, to swim across a pit of water means to escape a terrible situation. People frequently say of the Khmer Rouge period, for instance, *I swam through those years.*

For a while, I think of memory like swimming underwater. Its shadows fall the way light glimmers through waves, broken and formless; light, dark, light. Eventually there comes a moment, I think, when you have to rise for air. Eventually you come crashing through.

But it doesn't work like this. There's no crash, no through. More, memory closes itself off like a secret passage, and you swim through the lit rooms of yourself, forgetful and unafraid.

15. *come to*

To recover consciousness, wake, or (of a ship) come to a stop.

I faint and then I stop fainting. The ghost on my chest comes and goes.

My cousin tells me, almost in passing, *I'm going to visit my dad's grave.* Twenty years have passed since we studied her father inside his coffin. That she's going doesn't surprise me so much as the words themselves.

My dad.

In all the years of whispering in the dark, I never once heard her speak them.

Dara tells me that a few years after the fall of the Khmer Rouge, he won a scholarship to study in the Soviet Union. The most shocking things, he says, were the doors that would glide open right in front of you. He couldn't fathom the internal mechanism by which they opened and closed, and standing there in the airport, trying to make his way to the taxis outside, he was paralyzed. A group of young men saw him standing there—arms crossed, afraid. They told him the doors were magic: you had to say the magic word to get through. He stood there for what seemed like hours, trapped.

How did you get out?

I forgot all my Russian. I couldn't think of any word. So finally I looked down at my plane ticket and saw my own name. That's what I said as I walked through the door.

PHNOM PENH

We came as four but left one by one. We were replacements. We were girls.

Hi, New Girl.

Hi, New Girl Two.

This was the *Cambodia Daily*. This was news. We'd come to replace a dead girl. Or we'd come to replace three boys and a girl. (Always, it's the girl who dies.) The four of us, we knew nothing or we knew not to ask. We knew the headline from the local paper: *Foreign Reporter Dead.* We heard whispers about drugs, about the three boys in the room—fired or fled, we didn't know. We looked at each other and wondered who was who. Who were the boys, the dead girl, the ghost? Secretly, we all thought she was us.

We huddled around desks, elbows touching. We got shouted at. We got stares. We did everything wrong. On the street, we got offers. *Lady, tuk-tuk? Smoke-smoke? Killing Fields?* At the Killing Fields, we walked like sleepwalkers among the skulls—some smashed, some whole. The mud retched up a piece of cloth and we gasped. We'd believe anything: the dead coming up out of the ground. We all thought she was us. When the king died, we ran outside to see his face in the moon.

She died with her head tilted back. We knew her name. We knew not to ask. We learned Khmer from the local news. One of our first words: gang rape. *Bauk*. It was always in the paper—three boys and a girl. Or four boys, five. It happened all the time. We were told not to point at the moon: *Bad luck*. It happened all the time.

Which of us was the dead girl, the ghost? We crashed our motorcycles. We got into scrapes. We were too pretty or we were not pretty enough. We were too quiet. Too loud. We laughed at jokes—*Who put the hyphen in rape-murder?*—then cried in the bathroom. It happened all the time. We talked to the dead girl's ghost.

They fell in love with us. They hated us. We were sleeping with our bosses, our sources. We were sleeping with men from the other paper. We were probably sleeping with each other. They shouted. They stormed off and forgot to pay their tabs. We talked to the dead girl's ghost. Some of us fell in love with the ones who shouted most.

We called to report gossip. We called to ask what kind of mood he was in. At bars, we sat on the same stool, then shouted that we were not the same person. *But can I just point out that you're sitting on top of each other right now?* We debated the coming coup, jumped at dark spots scuttling across the floor. We fell in love with the ones who shouted most. The dead girl understood.

We kissed in tuk-tuks and drove through floods. We made human pyramids in bars. We lost all our money at the Chinese casino, then stumbled home drunk to make instant noodles at 3 a.m. The dead girl understood. We passed out in each other's beds whispering things we wouldn't remember.

They talked about us. Who was pretty. Who was fat. Who dressed like a ladyboy. Whose ass had that thing that made you want to look. We stayed late. We threw up in the bathroom. We never once called in sick. They called stories sexy and we hated it. They called stories sexy and we did it too. We said things we wouldn't remember. In the morning, we woke up hung over.

We got in with the right tuk-tuk drivers. We got into the right girly bars. We spotted license plates, eavesdropped in bars. We got invited to private islands. We got our fortunes told. In the morning, we woke up hung over. We were told we'd live a long time.

We slept with everyone. We slept with no one. We ignored messages and cried in the bathroom. We slept with someone finally just to prove that we could. We were told we'd live a long time. When he got up to walk through the kitchen, we pictured him grabbing a knife.

We fought about stories. We fought all the time. We fought about foreign pedophiles, about genocide. We said it would never happen at home. We said it happened all the time. We were too mad to leave together, then got robbed alone on the street: two men in the dark, and the dark was a knife. We screamed, but it didn't sound like our voice.

For weeks, we were bored. We counted murders, took bets on lightning strikes. Then one day we saw a man get shot dead right in front of us. We crouched behind the car while the shooters debated. We couldn't breathe. We couldn't remember the things we were supposed to remember. We couldn't remember our voice.

We no longer told each other everything. Instead, we sat at bars and embellished stories. Made up words. *Deathpat is like sexpat except you come here to shoot up and die.* We wondered if we were a kind of deathpat. *Maybe everyone who comes here is a kind of deathpat.* We were told not to stay too long. We were told to stay away from cocaine. It was two years, and we were still debating the coming coup. We wondered if all this would always seem real; already there were things we forgot.

We heard the story of the dead girl finally, but it wasn't what we'd thought. *Stupid girl. Everyone knows the coke here is all heroin.* We still believed we were her—the dead girl, the ghost—though now we sometimes thought we might live. Most of the people who'd known her had gone. Her name came up less. We talked to her now and then, but more often we forgot. We'd been told we'd live a long time.

We vowed to stop drinking or we didn't. We went to meetings or we didn't. We vowed to live our lives one day at a time. We ran. We bargained. We prayed. We prayed sick in our beds in the middle of the night. *Let me live and I swear I won't do this anymore.* We prayed not to be too quiet. Too loud. We stayed silent or we screamed at the top of our lungs. It never saved us or it did.

We told ourselves it was all right not to wear our helmets—something about the night in our hair, something about the tree blossoms hung with stars. We told ourselves no one had ever lived a life like this. We told ourselves we were bored. We told ourselves it was our voice, our scream—it was the silence that had belonged to someone else. It never saved us or it did. We told ourselves we'd live a long time.

YOUR VILLAGE HAS BEEN BOMBED

Dear citizens:

Your village has been bombed. The area demarcated in red on the map below displays a target zone of high enemy concentration. Your village, falling within this zone, is subject to strategic airstrikes of sublime and proportional magnitude, otherwise known as Death from the Sky. This leaflet, dropped from above, is neither an expression of regret nor a warning but a stating of terms: the enemy hides among you.

Dear citizens:

Below us, your village sprawls flat and legible as a manual. Your streets spiral in ancient calligraphy, your alleys etched like cuneiform. Near the village center, merchants peddle their dusty wares. Smoke curls up from your place of worship, its roof glinting in the sun. But there are smaller places of worship too—at least one for every house. We see you filing in and out of these places, praying and not praying, praying again. We wonder what it is you pray for.

Dear citizens:

We fly above your village under cover of cloudbanks. We sparkle it with lasers, and pictures stream back, dirt streets rising up at us, scanned and pixelated. We see you moving through these streets—on bicycles, on foot, behind cattle. We see you buying vegetables at the market. We see you at home, wiping the chins of your children. We see you reading this very leaflet. You must know that if the enemy hides in your house, your house will be destroyed. If the enemy hides in your fields, your fields will be destroyed. If the enemy hides inside you, traced along the very walls of your skin, we will destroy the walls, the trace.

Dear citizens:

At night, your village glows. It beams up to us a kind of radioactive blueprint, every little crevice evincing itself into night. Your heat signatures transmit tiny signals that shudder through the dark, and we watch you moving through unlit rooms. You pray or you don't pray. You turn in your sleep. To us, you look small as ants, crawling through a dream city. In truth, we are up here so long and so late, we sometimes think we are the ones dreaming you.

Dear citizens:

When we drop our payloads, time gets fast and also slow, a kind of temporal vertigo. Houses gibber into flames. Trees blaze quick as struck matches.

Afterward, we orbit your collapsed roofs. We see your shattered windows, your doors bent from the hinges. These things orbit inside us, but faintly, very faintly, and far. Far as our own deaths, locked in some future drawer. We see, just outside the blast radius, a small flung bicycle, its back wheel still spinning.

Dear citizens:

Hellfire, the stuff we drop is called. The old stuff was called Reaper. Some say it's the same stuff, with a new name.

Somebody asks: *Don't Hellfire mean you're already dead?*

Dear citizens:

Sometimes, on nights when it's quiet, we go into auto indefinite and just drift. Occasionally we go into auto infinite, though we're careful not to stay too long. Out there, you can come unmoored, become all drift. Spooking, they call this. In an old war, they called it Puffing, as in Puff the Magic Dragon, because of the way your mind warps through the clouds. It's a strange kind of rush, how you float outside yourself, tethered by only the faintest memory. How night pulls back like a curtain and time gets wide as light—everywhere, and everywhere at once. And then finally how you come hurtling out of it, the sky hooking you back into space, straight-time locking you in. For a second, the mind reels like a gear with no catch—an unearthly kind of turbulence. You wonder not who you are or even what, but how you are a *you* at all.

Dear citizens:

We blaze messages into the dirt—inside jokes, obscene renderings of army chants. *For a good time, call Wanda.* Who is Wanda? We don't know, but it kills us every time.

Sometimes, just before exploding them, we write our names into the walls of houses.

Dear citizens:

House by tiny house, your village diminishes. But still you move about, making your way through the charred streets. We see the black smoke of bombing and then the tiny dribbles of smoke which must be praying. We've heard you write the names of the dead on slips of paper and then burn them, that this is how prayers reach the afterlife.

Dear citizens:

Things come at us fast. Planes, birds, piteous homemade rockets. In these moments, our hands lurch toward the eject button. We have to stop each other. *Don't do it*, we say. *Don't.* Then afterward, we sigh, our hearts settling back down into our chests. *Almost just shit myself out of the sky.*

Dear citizens:

We take no pleasure in this. Or no, this is not true, exactly. There's always a certain pleasure in destruction. The smash-bang of it, the jolt and awe, the sheer visual flux—houses shuddering and then gone. It's not personal. It's never personal. It's just matter collapsing into dust. If the world makes and unmakes, we are merely siding with the unmaking. If time is entropy, we are merely creatures of time. It's hard sometimes, being time—ticking and ticking, never able to stop. A small bicycle wheel spins inside us.

Dear citizens:

There are no houses left to bomb, but still, at night, little blinks move through your cratered streets. What are these blinks? They are nowhere to be found in the Targeting and Collateral Damage Computational Handbook, which we have committed to memory. At first, we believed they were heat signatures going out in tiny flares. We believed, essentially, that these were the pinpricks of the dying, piercing through space. But even now, weeks later, the blinking continues. Some of us think it must be the bats that come out at night. Others say a glitch in the radar, a jammed signal. Still others say that the dead, like the living, have their own signature, always traced in absence.

These are the things we talk about in the dark, our voices, encrypted, traveling across the black night. We talk sometimes just to disturb the quiet. We admit things we'd rather not admit. We admit, for instance, that your tiny curved streets tug at us, that they remind us of other places, other streets, though we cannot recall where those streets might be.

Dear citizens:

The enemy has moved. The enemy is always moving. There are other villages, other streets. But still we come back to you. We drop leaflets, though you never answer us. We wonder if there's something we've missed—a blind spot in our periphery, a void at the center of seeing. Our sensors dilate and contract. We calibrate our electro-optics to the exact radius of the night. But we've begun to suspect that something has gone awry with the circuitry. An odd kind of static gets through. It garbles the space between seeing and seen.

We stare into your wrecked houses at night, peer into your bedrooms. It gets lonely up here, after all. We wonder: if you are not real, if you are just pinpricks, tiny holes in the universe, what is it you are holding onto in each other?

Dear citizens:

We laugh and joke and spook, but questions pull at us. We've begun to wonder if your village is even real. We wonder if real and unreal places assuage the same hungers. We look down at your village with its remaining stick trees. We wonder: what would happen if we pressed the eject button? Would we trapdoor into empty space, free fall through air? We picture it: the sound of engines, the rush of gravity. We dream of falling. It's the landing we can't quite conjure. Would we plummet down into a tiny bombed village, or would we emerge somewhere else entirely? Would we—*could* we—step out into the desert twenty miles from our homes, the tidy prefab houses where our children lie sleeping?

Dear citizens:

There's a story we faintly recall—perhaps a book we once read to our children? We can't remember. Sometimes it's hard to remember our children. Some faint smell of shampoo, tiny glowing heads of hair. We have to think these things are real. In the story, there's a lonely boy ghost haunting an old house. The children in the house can't see him. He talks to them, but they never hear. In the end, he's taken in by a family of ghosts, and you see him frolicking with his ghost brothers and sisters. We think of this boy ghost sometimes. We ask ourselves: who is it who can speak to ghosts?

Dear citizens:

Every twenty-four hours, our systems reboot. Our control panels go dark. Even the high-pitched little navigator quiets. In those moments, we think of our own deaths. Mostly we've always thought we'd manage to go dark slowly. We wouldn't go out like a flare. We wouldn't transmit like something too quick for words.

But we're no longer sure of such things. We're no longer sure of most things, in fact. We try to remember an equation: *a body in space falls at the rate of—*

Rate of what? We can't remember the word. *A body in space—*

Much later it comes to us, ambushes us in the dark: *gravity.* We've forgotten about gravity. We don't look down at our own bodies, afraid to think what we might see.

Dear citizens:

We continue to drop all the standard leaflets: *Your village has been bombed because you housed the enemy. Your village has been bombed because you fed the enemy. Your village has been bombed by the enemy.*

But now we rewrite these leaflets. We write and rewrite.

Before your village, there was another village. In this village, there once lived a boy who rode a bicycle. One day, he rode his bicycle straight into the radius of a bomb blast. Or no. There were two boys. They were brothers. The younger brother was watching. He watched his brother and he watched the blast and he understood that he would always be outside its radius. Or no. The truth is, there were many boys. Some of them grew up. Some of them didn't. Some turned themselves into the radius of a bomb blast. These are the things that recur.

Dear citizens:

A strange noise creeps through the dusk. It whines, hovers, slyly whisks through space—music. Strings and horns, the low roll of percussion. A veritable symphony rising up out of the trees. But how can this be? We were told you had no music.

You out there? Copy?

You hear that?

We hear it.

But how can—?

It can't.

They aren't supposed to—

They aren't *anymore.*

But we hear it.

A long pause.

You think if we'd've known—

Would we—?

Yeah.

Another pause.

No. Well—maybe.

The sky gets to that in-between light, night lifting up off the ground. Around us, a firmament of clouds. Things happen here and also there. Near and also far. Einstein called it spooky action at a distance. We wonder if these leaflets are their own type of spooky action—if words are always spooky action at a distance. Like burning the names of the dead so a prayer might reach them. Like talking to ghosts to make them real.

The music vibrates, hovers, plucks at something inside us. Faint as a small bicycle wheel still turning. These things unmake us. But then, we think, isn't that proof there was something to unmake?

Dear citizens:

We think of the eject button. We think of the door latched tight below us. There are two possibilities. In one, we open the door and fall through space, hurtle to our deaths. In the other, we open the door but don't fall through it. Instead, we stand up, dazed, in a bunker twenty miles from our homes. We get up, drive home to our children. (Why is it so hard to remember our children?)

Of course, there's a third possibility, but it's the one that's hardest to consider. The third possibility is that there's no we, no door.

Say you live in a vessel so long, you don't know where it ends and you begin. Say you manipulate its controls seamlessly, each movement quick and sure as a pulse. How would you know, then—how would you know what you'd find on the other side of the door?

Dear citizens:

In the negative space left by your village, a new village becomes visible. The Village That Is No Longer, or maybe the Village That Never Was. What is the space between these two villages? In it, there are people wandering through streets. They buy vegetables at the market. They wipe the chins of their children. Two small boys ride a bicycle, one pedaling, one perched atop the handlebars. One is telling the other a story about a ghost—a lonely boy ghost who no one can hear.

We dream about these villages, the one that was and the one that was never. We think of our own children, asleep between their tiny prefab walls. We think of that riddle from childhood: *If a body falls in a dream and there's no one awake to hear it, does it still make a sound?*

Dear citizens:

We're doing it. We're pressing the eject button. We don't know where we'll fall to. We don't know if we'll fall. We don't know if we'll go out in a flare or flicker out dark. Maybe we'll transmit like something too quick for words. Or maybe in this transmitting, we'll become briefly legible. Citizens, this is not a stating of terms, though it is a kind of plea. Pray for us. Our names are written on your walls.

EDIE

I.

This was the year Edie was an alien, the year I met Edie. We'd sit hunched between pine trees, solemn and twitchy with waiting. This was the year we were always waiting. Any minute might be the minute. Any sound the sound. It was coming: a blast of light, a message beamed down, the thrum of transmission moving across the trees. Just wait, said Edie. Just wait.

And I did wait. A person could believe anything around Edie. Edie who careened across the monkey bars—a flash, a shriek, a body flung from too-high places. Edie who stuck a finger in the air and declared the atmosphere poison: only aliens could breathe. Edie, the bane of teachers and lunch aides, always in trouble. Edie who watched from up high as the rest of us held our breath and heaved.

Edie who looked like an ordinary girl but was not. She slid her hair back and forth across her head: a wig, she said. Edie who spun around in front of me in line, pulled down the lower lid of her eye. "Look," she commanded.

Always, I turned away. I didn't like to see the insides of people, wet and red. Blood made me sick, just the thought of it. How much there was. And how flimsy the skin holding it back.

"Just *look*."

And then I would look. I'd look straight into Edie's inner eye: the squirm of white in its socket, the bright larval red. Inside, she said, were three white dots—tiny alien cells hatched inside her. I'd look and look, unseeing, until something lurched inside my stomach and the floor rolled beneath me. And then for a second, I did see: tiny bright specks, quivery with the light of far-off stars.

Truthfully, I'd known about Edie a whole year before I met her. In first grade, our classrooms were adjacent, connected by a shared bathroom. With the doors shut, it was easy to imagine your classroom a world of its own, a tight, locked capsule—nothing before or after, nothing outside it. But every now and then, by chance, the doors on either side were left open, and through them, you'd catch a glimpse of a kind of parallel universe: bright, shiny posters, little clusters of desks. A world at once familiar and strange, rearranged like in a dream.

Then one day, I looked through the doors and saw Edie. She'd crawled up onto her desk and stood there, teetering with rage. The teacher spit the hard syllables of her name—her full name, *Edith*, which even I knew was wrong—and a tremor went through Edie like a struck nail. She spun toward the voice, her face bright with fury, and I could see she was shouting, though I didn't hear a single word. I was too overcome by the sight of her, a sight so strange and out of the ordinary, it unturned something inside me. You weren't allowed to stand on your desk. You especially weren't allowed to stand on your desk and shout at the teacher.

Edie was nothing like me. I was sunken, shy, so quiet I was practically mute. But I felt something watching her. She was the answer to an unasked question—a clue, a signal, the key that turned the quiet in me. She was a force all her own, a planet unsprung from her orbit and hurtling toward mine.

So when, on the first day of second grade, she asked me to come wait for aliens in the trees, I didn't ask questions. Because I'd waited for Edie too, watched her from across the playground. I'd watched and waited and one day she was there.

Our town was famous but not to us. We understood, faintly, that it appeared in history books, that zealous day-trippers came armed with maps looking for clues, answers to the famous kidnapping. This was the thing we were famous for: a toddler in the woods, dug up and dead. The pilot's kidnapped son.

There was a girl in our class whose grandfather had been the one to find it, the dead and kidnapped baby. He was the town milkman, stopping his truck to go pee in the woods. What he found was dirty and decomposing, dug up by animals—the nightgown disintegrated, the skull cracked in. But even so, he knew it was a human, a kid.

This was the year we studied Indians in school. This was the year we studied the famous dead baby. All this was the history of our town. The Lenapes, long disappeared. The baby, who'd disappeared too. We sat at our desks filling out worksheet after worksheet. *What foods did the Lenapes eat? What sort of crafts did they make?* We studied floor plans, positioned and repositioned the ladder up to the nursery. We read a story about a girl kidnapped by Indians and renamed Corn Tassel. "Lucky," said Edie.

Soon our class was going on a field trip to the pilot's house. Even the thought of it roused a skittish electricity inside us. We ran crazy around the room, flung our bodies against walls. "I'll kidnap you," we told each other. "I'll ransom your kidnapped bones."

The boys, especially, liked the story of the milkman. "Did he pee on it?" every boy wanted to know. "Did he pee on the dead baby?" This was also the year of dead baby jokes: dead babies and microwaves, dead babies and blenders, dead babies and all manner of kitchen appliances. "Bet he did pee on it," the boys answered their own question. "Bet he *definitely* peed on it."

At this, the milkman's granddaughter would start to cry. Her name was Beth, and we were supposed to be nice to her. There was something in her brain, a kind of growth, though she looked no different from the rest of us—only cried too easily and picked her nose and sometimes stole people's lunches out of the coatroom. Probably she made it all up, the boys said. Probably her grandpa hadn't even found the baby. Probably *he* was the one who killed it in the first place.

Beth came to school every day wearing two different-colored socks. This had been one of Edie's rules. If you wanted to be an alien, she'd announced the first week of second grade, you had to wear mismatched socks. But this was only one rule of many. Aliens didn't wear skirts or dresses. Aliens stepped only on black tiles in the hall. Aliens picked the pepperoni off their pizza and preferred chocolate milk at lunch. The rules, however, were subject to change, and Edie hadn't worn mismatched socks since September. Now it was almost Halloween—I was going as Pocahontas, Edie as the Grim Reaper— and every girl in the second grade had adjusted her footwear accordingly. Every girl except Beth.

I'd worn mismatched socks only grudgingly. I didn't want to be like all the other girls. I didn't like to admit to wanting to be Edie. Or, it wasn't that I wanted to be her, exactly. What I wanted was to watch as she flung herself from the monkey bars or shouted from her desk—to look and look until there was no difference between seeing and being.

Some days I walked home from school and told myself I didn't even believe Edie. I wasn't like the other girls, convinced by her dumb wig trick, her litany of rules. But the minute I was near her, I believed all over again. Belief wasn't one thing or the other, I began to see, but fickle and strange, like weather. All you could do was watch while its wide, blowing clouds moved past.

•

It was the day before the field trip, and we were watching from between the trees—Edie pointing, our heads tilted back. "Look," said Edie. I saw branches, leaves. Bits of blue. Some days I was sure I could feel it: the air alive, transmitting. A shadow at the edge of my eye—something too close to see. All around us, we laid out pine needles. There was a right number, a right pattern—a pattern known only to Edie. I wobbled my loose tooth with my tongue.

Aliens didn't have bodies, Edie said. At least not the kind humans could see. But the more she said I couldn't, the more I saw: strange bulbous life-forms with long needles in their hands. In these visions, I saw Edie laid out still as a doll below. I saw the jellyfish goop of her insides, the blood and gush of her. She looked to me like the plastic body in Operation, her organs waiting to be extracted one by one.

What was it like? I was always asking. What did it feel like?

"Not like anything," Edie would say. "Not *like* at all."

But once, out of nowhere, she whispered that she'd felt a painless sort of cutting—a glowy itch creeping up her abdomen.

"Tell me again," I said now. "Please."

Sometimes I thought Edie was protecting me. I was a human, a girl. I was weak and killable. But other days, I was sure she was guarding her alien life—a secret so thrilling and beautiful she didn't want to share it. I pictured how the Earth would look from up high, a tiny dropped ball marbled with color. And how it would feel to see everything you'd ever known—a bright round moment, the whole world all at once.

"It's hard to explain to Earthlings."

"So show me."

"Show you what?"

"Make me alien."

There was a look in Edie's eyes—a blankness, like she'd disappeared behind her own face. Then all at once, she was running, slipping through the cage of pine trees, and I knew I was supposed to follow. Branches snagged my hair. Needles pricked my skin. All this was Edie's territory, the woods and field. She was always collecting pieces of it: rocks, snakeskin, bones. Evidence.

Now she stopped short. Before us lay a dead deer, its ribs bashed in, a mess of fur and blood. In the distance, we could hear the road where it must have limped from, a jet stream of cars moving just past the trees.

"At least it got to die in the woods," said Edie. We lived in a town of dead deer—dead deer on roadsides, in ditches, spray-painted with bright orange *X*'s—and more than anything, Edie hated seeing them on the road. It had to do with dead animal spirits, which she was highly attuned to. Sometimes, sitting in the back of my mother's station wagon, we'd pass over the mossy smudge of something dead, and Edie would insist that we both hold our breath so its animal spirit would race through us a little longer.

Now she said solemnly, "That's the way it goes." This was another habit of Edie's: adopting the odd phrases of grown-ups and TV sitcoms. Always it unsettled me. "Sounds like a plan," Edie'd say on the phone, hanging up, and I'd stare into the receiver wondering: *Who are you?* Because Edie couldn't be like anyone else, and certainly she couldn't be a jumble of used-up words. I preferred to think of her as sprung fully formed from thin air, instantaneous and new. A tiny magician pulled from her own hat.

But this was only one of the many puzzle pieces of Edie, small mysteries I turned over and over in my brain. There was the way she could be affectionate one minute and distant the next, embarrassed by even the smallest of intimacies. No one was allowed to touch her,

and especially not her hair. "What about a little braid?" girls sometimes tried. I'd watch these exchanges, amused, knowing what came
next: Edie screaming right in their ears.

Her house was its own mystery—its stewy smells, its grass up
to my knees. Rusted appliances sprouted from the lawn like giant
baffled weeds. An old shed sat rotting out back, but the one time I'd
asked if we could play in it, Edie shook her head no. "My brother and
sister are having sex in there," she said, shrugging.

Edie's sister was six; her brother, seven. I said the only thing I
could think of: "That's impossible."

"I know," said Edie. "I *told* them that."

In the soft dirt by the cellar, Edie kept her box of evidence, which
we buried and unburied. Sometimes the dirt turned up other things:
a piece of glass, a kitchen knife, limbs of a Barbie brutally assassi-
nated. At Edie's house, not even the ground beneath my feet felt sure
or solid. Everything was always colliding into everything else: people
and smells and limbs, unknowable things coming up out of the dirt.
Always when I left, I was glad to be back on hard ground.

"That's the way it goes," Edie said again, but quieter this time.
And then, without warning, she sprinted ahead. We ran and ran and
kept running, then finally broke through to the stunned open field.
Cold stung my eyes.

In the night, a freeze had come and cratered the field with ice, a
shiny moonscape we slid across. I knew by then where we were going. At the far edge of the field sat a bathtub, cracked up the middle,
like something plunked down out of the sky. Edie said it was from
the old orphanage, burnt up in a fire. We liked to sit inside and make
the field around us an ocean, a fire, an alien terrain. We'd float up
above, so high we could see everything: our houses growing smaller, our streets folded up between hills. We saw the hills, dark and
dreamy. The high-up turns that sometimes reared up late at night,

shucked cars of teenagers down into the trees. Once, Edie said the bathtub was a spaceship and a spaceship could travel at the speed of light, past hours, years. "Which," she said, "proves time isn't real." And from up high, I could see it was true: I saw the houses unmade, the roads spooled in, the orphans burning in their beds. We watched the world end, saw it flooded and ravished and burned, did it again.

Now Edie pursed her lips. "Get in."

Inside the bathtub were pebbles, dirt. Two dead flies, stunned and quiet. I looked up at her. "Aren't you coming too?"

"Close your eyes."

I shut one eye and watched through the eyelashes of the other.

"Ruthie, you have to close *both*."

With my eyes closed, I could feel things I hadn't before. The dark coming up out of the ground, night rising like water above my head. The sound the wind made moving through the trees. Then I felt Edie's hands crawling over my jacket. Her hands walked up my limbs and onto my chest. There was the faintest of noises, like buzzing, and I pictured the flies stirring beside me, resurrected. It was the slippery light between night and day, and anything could happen: dead things sprung to life, a girl made alien.

A quiet came, and Edie's hands went cold and still at my neck. I opened my eyes and saw her face hovering close to mine. I felt her breath hot on my cheek. But her gaze was an odd, unseeing sort of stare: like I was a stranger, someone she'd never known.

"Edie," I said, suddenly afraid. A bit of my jaw had come loose inside my mouth. For a second it was terrifying; I was losing a piece of myself. Then it dropped smooth and white into my hand—a tooth.

We leaned in to stare at its glittery-hard smoothness, its jagged underside and dot of blood. "Can I have it?" asked Edie.

"No." I clasped the tooth to my chest. It was mine, it was *me*. I didn't want to let it go.

"You can still get money. Just tell your mom it fell out in the woods."

Days earlier, playing in Edie's yard, we were called into the kitchen by her father. When he saw me, saw the tooth I couldn't stop wobbling, he said, "Hey, come over here and let me get that tooth out for you. We'll tie it here"—he'd rattled the doorknob—"and get it right out."

I'd stood there frozen, my heart going crazy in my chest. I didn't know if he meant it, if he really meant to pull the tooth from my head, but it seemed possible: anything was possible at Edie's house. The outlines slippery, everything colliding into everything else. I felt at that moment that Edie's dad could stick his hand inside me, pull my insides up and out through my throat, and I felt too that I'd have to let him, a kind of dream gravity pinning my feet to the ground. It was at this moment that Edie reached out and grabbed my hand—the first time I'd ever known her to break her rule about touching. She pulled me across the backyard, toward the sidewalk, and it felt for a moment like we were being chased—by the rattling doorknob, by the house, by slippery fears we couldn't speak. Edie understood my fear—or maybe it was *her* fear inside me—and I knew at that moment that I'd follow her anywhere.

Now, in the bathtub, blood's slow trickle tasted hot and ancient in my mouth. "Why?" I asked, still holding tight to my tooth.

"Because my collection is only animal bones. Nothing human. Your tooth could be famous in another galaxy."

For once it seemed I held a kind of power over Edie—Edie who zipped back and forth across outer space, Edie who'd gone from girl to alien. What she wanted was so tiny and human: a tooth. A tooth I'd done nothing at all to acquire, which simply grew in my head and then one day fell out. "I'll trade you," I said finally. "But you have to promise. Promise you'll take me with you."

Edie was quiet, but I knew I didn't need to explain.

"Please." I was still a girl, a body with its loose teeth, its breakable parts. But Edie could take me in her spaceship nonetheless. She could take me with her.

Edie's eyes met mine. "Okay. Promise."

Night was a giant blue dome dropped all around us. It erased our faces first, then our fingers and limbs. The dark moved us across the field, and for a moment I had no body at all. Edie and I moved apart, then together again, dark spots blown across the moon. I touched the new hole in my mouth, fleshy and smooth, and pictured my tooth hurtling through all the dark of outer space—jagged and bright and clasped in Edie's hand.

The morning of the field trip to the pilot's house, we lined up in pairs on the blacktop. Edie chose me, and I sighed with secret relief. You never knew with Edie. Out of nowhere, her eyes could turn cruel and ruthless, and she'd leave you stranded on the playground like you'd never once met. One recess, I'd watched as she pranced around a group of girls like a fairy godmother, wielding a stick for a wand. She'd chanted: "I make thee more beautiful, more beautiful." When she got to her ex-best friend, a fat and freckled girl named Caitlin, she stopped and said, "I make thee beautiful."

All week, Edie had been jumpy and excitable, even more than the rest of us, every morning asking Mrs. Griswold how many days before the field trip. On the bus, I finally understood why. She had a theory. Edie had a theory for many things: light, time, diving bell spiders. The latest involved aliens. How could a human have found the pilot's house? she wanted to know. It was too well hidden in the woods, and besides that, there was the matter of the ladder. A human couldn't have known the exact location of the nursery.

No, said Edie, it had to be aliens. When they dropped the baby back to Earth, they'd meant for him to be intact and sleeping. What

happened was a misjudgment, a mishap: human kids were too fragile. In the end, it was easy to make it look like a kidnapping since kids
got stolen all the time.

I tugged at the bus seat's torn vinyl, which smelled faintly of
vomit. "But why would aliens leave a ransom note?"

"They *had* to," said Edie. "They had to throw the cops off the trail."

Right then, Edie held her breath and closed her eyes, so I closed
my eyes too.

"Hey, look." Dan Butler splat his hand against the window behind us. "Roadkill."

Before I could say anything, Edie had climbed up onto the seat
beside me and grabbed him by his hair. She hated the word *roadkill.*
"Take it back, Barf Breath."

"Take it back or *what?*"

"Take it back or I'll slit your fat stupid throat."

"Okay, I take it back. *God.*"

The bus lurched forward. At every turn, Edie and I elbowed each
other in the ribs. "Sorry," I said each time. "Sorry." A guard had to let
us through a metal gate, and then we came up a long gravel driveway.
At the top of a hill sat a sprawling old house. A group of teenage
boys, all black, were raking leaves into piles. Mrs. Griswold had explained about these boys. Residents, she called them. The property,
she said, had been given to the state to make a home for boys in
trouble with the law.

"What about their parents?" Max Hullfish asked.

"They'll go back to their parents," Mrs. Griswold assured him.
"It's only temporary. Like summer camp."

Edie raised her hand. "Probably some of them are murderers."

"That's not the case, Edie," said Mrs. Griswold.

Now the residents stopped raking and watched us, our class
trundling one by one off the bus. The residents were a strange sight

in our town. Our class was white—our town, our school. There was one black fourth-grader; his dad was the janitor. Every morning they drove in from Trenton, and always he was first on the playground, surveying the empty parking lot from the Eagle's Perch.

But suddenly, at the pilot's house, it was different. As though the town's every black resident had been secreted away to this one hilltop.

"Murderers," Edie whispered, not in fear but in awe. Mostly our classmates stole sideways glances at the residents, but Edie stared unabashedly. She walked past a pile of raked leaves, swerved at the last moment and kicked, dead leaves flying behind her.

"Edie," gasped Mrs. Griswold. "Apologize."

"Sorry," said Edie, though she didn't look sorry at all. Mrs. Griswold turned and apologized on Edie's behalf—she was mortified, just mortified.

But I knew Edie only wanted to prove herself, to mark herself different. The rest of us, we were susceptible to kidnappers and killers. Our limbs weak, our skulls fragile. But not Edie, who had been to space and come out the other side—inhuman and unafraid.

From the house emerged a fat and pinkish man in a bowtie, trailed by a tall, solemn-faced resident. The bowtied man introduced himself as Ralph and gave a short speech about the house, the pilot, the crime of the century. But my eyes kept drifting instead to the resident, who stooped a little as if to apologize for his height and winced only slightly when Ralph clapped him on the shoulder. "I'd like to introduce you all to Andre," Ralph said. "He'll be giving you the grand tour."

Andre nodded, then went around and shook each and every one of our hands. When he got to Edie, he shook her hand and remarked admiringly, "You've got a grip there." Edie beamed. For the millionth time, Mrs. Griswold reminded us about bus buddies.

We toured the downstairs first, its perfectly preserved rooms and high arched ceilings. As we walked, Andre recited a long list of facts about the pilot—his early barnstorming flights, his solo trips across the ocean.

Edie squirmed beside me. She didn't care about any of this. What she wanted was to get to the nursery.

At every pause, Andre was met with a barrage of questions—none about the pilot. Did Andre really live here? Was it haunted? Did he get to eat dessert?

I had a question about the pilot, but I was too afraid to ask it. I wanted to ask if it was true he'd hated Jews, which was what my father had told me. I was the only Jew in my class, and when my parents were asked to come give a talk about Hanukkah, everyone stared, silent and baffled. Everyone except John Bierbauer, who pointed at the menorah and said, "My mom had one of those, but my dad ran it over with his truck."

Lately, I'd been going through a Holocaust phase. I'd read a book in which a girl fell through a portal in time and landed in a concentration camp. Since then I'd been dreaming about ovens and bodies, goose-stepping Nazis, and some nights I dreamt they were coming for me. In these dreams, I'd realize there was something on my body that gave me away—a Star of David necklace, a kind of foreignness about my face—and always this realization came too late.

"What about your parents?" Max Hullfish was asking Andre now. "Don't you miss your mom?"

Andre considered this. "I call her every Sunday."

"I'd miss *my* mom."

Edie shot Max a disdainful look. "Don't be such a *baby*." Turning to Andre, she bragged: "I never miss anyone. Even in outer space."

I looked at Edie and felt a distance of many light years trapped inside my chest. In my mind, I could still see a fast and gleaming spaceship. I could see Edie flown away inside it. Only I saw finally that I wasn't going with her, that she'd never meant to take me. I saw myself as she might see me, growing smaller and smaller in the distance. It was the same shrinking feeling that came over me the days she ignored me at recess, when she pretended not to know me, like I'd never once existed—worse, even, than the days she let me breathe poisoned atmosphere, when at least I'd been alive.

It was after we passed through a series of dark-paneled hallways that we stumbled out, squinting, into the courtyard's cold light. The tour, said Andre, would now be moving on to the grounds, to the gardens and tennis courts.

"Ruthie," Edie hissed. She was standing back, half-hidden in the doorway. "They're not taking us upstairs."

I shrugged, still hurt. "So?"

"So how are we going to see the window?"

"We won't, I guess."

"We *have* to."

Before I could answer, Edie'd turned and disappeared inside the house. Like always, I followed, hating that she knew I would. By the time I'd caught up, I could see just her feet disappearing up the stairs. The hall smelled of old, polished things, and I could hear the voices of our classmates growing small and tinny in the distance. Before, surrounded by the loudness of the others, I hadn't stopped to consider the fact that the pilot once lived here, once walked these very rooms. But now, alone in the hallway, I pictured him, and when I did, I saw him the way I saw Hitler in my mind: small and green and cutting off people's heads. I knew this wasn't how Hitler really looked, but it was the way I'd first imagined him and it had stuck. Now I saw a murderous green Nazi circling in his plane, and I knew suddenly that I was trapped—trapped in a house kids got stolen from, a house that now locked them in. "Edie," I whispered, loud as I could.

I had a trick for fear. When I felt myself slipping toward panic, I could crawl inside a word and stay there for whole minutes at a time. The first time it happened by accident. I was lying awake in bed one night when suddenly, for no reason at all, I seemed to be moving backward, sliding through the dark recesses of my head. My head itself was growing wider, expanding to fill the whole room, the house, the blue-black cosmos pricked with light. Below me, my body was small and distant, yet I was still somehow tethered to it, floating in the far reaches of my skull. The universe was edgeless and unspeakable and it was lodged inside my head.

In the days that followed, I went to bed earlier and earlier, hoping to summon it up again. But the universe never appeared to me in quite the same way. At most I could catch a sideways glimpse of it. I'd latch onto something in my head—a word was best—letting it swell wider and wider until I felt the stunned glimmer of something formless and huge: a darkness that wobbled, glinted.

Now it was the sound of my own whisper, *Edie*, rattling in my brain. Edie's name grew so big, it broke apart, drifted into syllables and sounds. They said and unsaid themselves until they were nothing at all, the universe pooling cold and silent at the base of my skull. I placed one foot on the stair in front of me and waited. The universe said nothing. I went up and up.

Upstairs was different right away. A carpet, thick and rubbery, a pair of Adidas left out in the hall. I found Edie staring up at a moss-colored wall in what appeared to be a game room: there was an air hockey table, a half-finished game of Connect Four. A worn Chutes and Ladders piece crunched beneath my foot—a cardboard girl with bright blonde pigtails and a missing tooth. I picked it up and squeezed it in my palm.

"This is it," said Edie. "This is the room." She pointed to the pastel tiles above the fireplace—one painted with a rocking horse, another with a teddy bear.

Edie, we'll get in trouble, said my brain, but when I opened my mouth, no sound came out. Instead I heard Edie's voice, telling me to come help. She was at the window, trying to pry it open, and for a second, I wondered if she'd push me out, just to prove her theory. But even with the two of us, the window refused to budge. I pressed my forehead to the glass. I could see our class in the distance, a clump of bright, moving ants. Beyond them, the hills were going brown. A flock of geese winged across the trees. I pictured the kidnapped baby flown off by aliens in the night. "Lucky," I whispered.

A voice came from the door. "Can I play?" It was Beth. She'd followed us.

"Go away," said Edie. "Only aliens here."

Beth grinned her dopey grin. "*I* want to be an alien."

"You can't," said Edie. "Aliens don't have cracked brains."

Beth's face scrunched up, and I could see the cry rising in her chest. "Shhh," I whispered. All of a sudden, I hated Beth—hated her Velcro shoes and dumb crying face. I hated most of all the way she walked down stairs, feet meeting together each time.

"Hey, look."

The voice made me jump. In the door stood two residents. They stared at us, then at each other. "Tour-group babies got in the rec room."

"We're not doing anything," I said.

The residents looked warily at Beth, her face streaked with snot. "She okay?" asked one, and I saw suddenly that he was afraid. It wasn't a fear I understood except to know that I was a part of it, that me and Edie and even Beth wielded a strange power here. We would leave this house, but the boys would stay and stay.

Edie looked at Beth and shrugged. "She's just sad because her granddad kidnapped the baby."

At this, Beth choked on a sob. She dropped to the floor and sank her head between her knees. Her socks stuck out like tongues from her jeans: one striped, one pink with tiny red hearts. An unnameable sadness flooded my chest. The word *kidnap* rattled in my skull, and I heard my own voice out in the trees: *Take me with you. Please.* A word could do things to you—just a word. It could hold you tight, refuse to let go. Because for a minute, I knew what it was like to be kidnapped. Knew what it was like for terror to reach its long arm through the universe and grab you. It was the dream I kept having, the one where something was coming for me—monsters, strange men, marching Nazis. Something whose word I couldn't know. And I saw too that there'd be no rising up beautifully above the Earth. No being spirited to a planet of many moons. But how trapped you'd be, how caught, pinned to your stupid dumb body as someone carried it off into the distance. It would split you in two.

Beth's hand, when I took it, was warm and sweaty in mine. "He didn't," I told her, though I was looking only at Edie. "It didn't have anything to do with you."

We were reproached for wandering off, though only lightly. Edie insisted we'd gone to help Beth, who'd wandered off on her own, and we rejoined the class waiting outside for the bus, each allowed to take a soda from the giant cooler.

Edie frowned at my Sprite. "Aliens drink Dr. Pepper."

I looked at her and felt something cold and ruthless stir in me. "Then I guess I'm not an alien," I said.

I stood off to the side, alone. I could hear Edie bragging about all the things we'd seen: trapdoors, secret passages, dungeons where bad kids were locked up. Finally the bus crested over the hillside like a hideous plastic sun. Edie made a point of sitting next to Sarah Mitchell, and I chose an empty two seater, not protesting when Max Hullfish sat down next to me. I shoved in toward the window and kept my torso stiff and straight each time we turned, not leaning toward anyone, not once.

Outside, a light rain was falling, and our breath turned the windows opaque with steam. My fingernails made tiny incisions in the glass, and I watched the world rush in, dense and sharp. The bus careened down the hills, a tight locked capsule, and I was the only one in the whole world who could see out.

I remembered the cardboard girl, shoved on a whim in my pocket, and now I held her in my hand, small and flimsy and grinning. "Go away," I mouthed, slipping her through the small opening in the window and watching as the wind rocketed her back—a tiny body punted through space. I pictured how the world would look falling away—a small falling object growing smaller. How for a minute you'd see everything, everything that had once been alive to you.

II.

The weather changed, the days grew shorter, and for a while Edie became a human girl again. No one mentioned aliens for the rest of second grade. Edie and I stayed friends, but it wasn't like before. That summer, she was shipped off to stay with her grandmother, whom she barely knew but already hated. We promised to write each other every day, settled on a secret code, but it wasn't until midway through August that I finally received a letter.

Dear Ruthie,

Sorry I haven't wrote you yet. It's totally barfy here let me give you a report. AHEM:

Yesterday while playing Monopoly my brother barfed and then my sister barfed on Grandma's head. (That was about the only good thing) And you wouldn't believe how many times Grandma has barfed (well knowing about her you might)—65 million times a day!

Your friend,
Edie
P.S. Thank you for the feather.

By the time Edie returned at the end of August, her mother had moved their belongings into a tiny apartment across town and her father was gone. I never knew what *gone* meant, exactly—if he'd left town or if he was just now absent from her life—but Edie never mentioned him again.

Third grade was the year of horses, girls penciling names like Misty and Cinnamon across their notebooks. Not Edie, of course. Edie began sitting at the boys' table at lunch, and boys had their own games—seeing who could eat the worst cafeteria concoction without puking, for instance. Edie always won.

Fourth grade was friendship bracelets: endless looping and knotting, threads strung to toes. I drifted between best friends, none of whom I felt as I had about Edie. Sometimes I'd try to get them to play along with something outlandish: witches, sea monsters, far-off planets. "You're so crazy, Ruth," they said admiringly. "What imagination," said their mothers. But it all felt too easy, a performance overly rehearsed.

Edie no longer ruled the playground, no legion of girls followed after her, but she still wielded her own kind of power. We rarely spoke, but every now and then she dropped into my life unexpectedly. Once we happened to walk into the girls' bathroom at the same time, and Edie motioned for me to be quiet. There was a noise in the far stall: a shuffling followed by a giant splash. Out walked Allison McDougal, the girl who'd spent the year insulting my clothes, my glasses, my every choice of words. She was one of the Prissy Girls, as I thought of them, but a peripheral member, thus necessitating a constant display of meanness.

I couldn't tell if Edie knew all this, but she walked straight up to Allison and said, "Hi, Pooper."

For a second, Allison stood there, stunned and frozen. Then she ran out into the hall.

For the rest of fourth grade, Edie kept it up. "Hi, Pooper," she'd call across the blacktop at recess.

"That's *not* my name," Allison would hiss. Once, I saw her turn away, tears in her eyes. It gave me a tiny thrill to know someone who could make Allison McDougal cry. She now avoided me at all costs, as though I'd brought the curse of Edie upon her.

By fifth grade, boys were divided into two ballgames at recess: soccer for the ones whose parents could afford travel leagues, kickball for the others. Outcast boys had their own games—Dungeons and Dragons, Magic: The Gathering.

Every girl game, however, had suddenly become about boys. There were girls who stalked the perimeter of the ballgames, watching. There were girls who paged through magazines with the devotion of scholars. They debated shades of lip gloss and which kinds boys liked best. They drew up endless games of MASH, spiraling out their futures—who they would marry and which kind of house.

In all this, Edie and I were both adrift, unmoored. One day in math class, we were solving a problem involving clocks and trains when she leaned across my desk. "I don't know how to tell time," she whispered. At first I thought this was a game I didn't understand, a joke. Because how could you get all the way to fifth grade without learning to tell time? Especially Edie, who never did her homework but scored the highest on every test. But then I saw she was serious, embarrassed by the clock she couldn't make sense of. "Well," I said, "time's not real anyway, right?"

Edie looked at me blankly.

So I told her it didn't matter about telling time. "Just ask me," I said. "Just ask and I'll tell the time for you."

And then we were friends again. We spent recesses penning an epic novel and plotting out film scripts. Edie's mom had remarried, and they'd moved again—this time to a big, new house with wall-to-wall carpets and a giant TV. Edie's stepdad had a camcorder, which we used to shoot movies in the basement: music videos, mockumentaries, talk shows. Mostly, I played the straight man to Edie's parade of characters: a deranged heiress who kept tennis balls in her bra, a member of a fantastically bad death metal band.

Sometimes we recruited additional actors. At Edie's sleepover birthday party, we assigned parts to all the girls, and they swirled around the basement trying on costumes and practicing their lines. Edie and I, meanwhile, sat huddled in the corner, scribbling amidst the chaos, and for a second I thought that I'd never been happier.

But the wonder of fifth grade was short-lived. The next year, Edie became briefly popular. It didn't last: she was asked out by a popular boy, and when they broke up, she was ejected from her seat at the popular table. Boys gave you a kind of power for a while, and then they didn't. Then you were just a slut. *Slut* was a word like *sex*, a wide and depthless black hole—I was afraid to look too close. Edie returned to my table of middle-tier girls, but it was different now. For one thing, she kept going out with boys—something that shocked me, though I couldn't say exactly why. By sixth grade, it had become clear that this was what some girls did. It just never occurred to me that Edie might be one of them. Sometimes she stood whispering in the hall with Lisa Corey, widely known as the sluttiest girl in our grade. They'd lean their heads close, discussing secret things, then stop talking when I came too near.

Still, Edie sometimes appeared in my doorway after dinner. She never came in, only said, "Can Ruthie come outside?" Edie was the only one who still called me Ruthie.

My parents were always happy to see her, like a long-lost friend, but she never accepted their offers of dinner or dessert. "We've missed you, Edie," they said, and Edie would look abashed and a little mournful as she glanced inside, as though she no longer belonged there. Sometimes, in these moments, I wondered if it wasn't me Edie wanted to be near but the settled trappings of my life.

Together, we'd walk around the park's steep edge—the cliff, we called it. From there, we could see Edie's house. At night, Edie's stepdad was known to fly into rages, and Edie liked to be close enough to keep an eye on things. Recently, she'd come to school with chips of paint stuck in the back of her head. "What happened?" I asked.

She ignored me, but her sister told someone who told someone else: Edie'd gotten thrown against a wall. For weeks, I kept seeing it in my head—Edie's small flung body, the sound her skull made against the wall. But though I tried, I could never quite picture the arms that picked her up and threw her. I couldn't picture any man doing such a thing, let alone Edie's stepdad, Larry, who always seemed warm and jovial. But like always, Edie had loosened the fixed points of the world, made its topography formless and wild. From the outside, Edie's house looked just like mine, which meant I could never be certain about anything.

One night in seventh grade, sitting on the cliff, Edie told me the most she ever did. "There's going to be a big explosion tonight," she said.

"How do you know?"

"Because Larry's going to wake up and see I painted *Die* in giant red letters on his door."

It had to do with Micah, Edie explained. Micah was Edie's youngest brother, who had Down syndrome. He was born just after her mother remarried, and he was the only person I ever saw Edie love fiercely and without hesitation. He could walk, but Edie liked to carry him around on her back, whispering over her shoulder, and sometimes they spoke to each other in a sign language part real, part secret. Once, I heard Edie murmur: "You're a little alien, like me."

It had jolted me, this mention of alienness, and then I was sure I'd heard wrong. Edie hadn't talked about aliens since second grade. Since then, our days of waiting in the trees had grown wispy to me. When I tried to remember what it was we had or hadn't seen, there was only a kind of hovering dark spot, shaky and formless, like after staring too long at something bright.

Now, on the cliff, Edie told me how Micah kept having accidents. He could use the bathroom, but sometimes he forgot or didn't notice until it was too late. Earlier in the night, in a rage, Larry had hosed him down outside in the cold as he screamed—a scream, said Edie, like he was being killed, like he was dying.

I thought for the first time in years about the pilot and his house. There was a whisper in town, just a whisper, that he was the real kidnapper, that he'd abducted and killed his own child.

"So I had to," Edie concluded. "Eye for an eye." Besides painting *Die*, she had also apparently printed out sheets of tiny Hitler faces from the Internet and pasted them onto Larry's face in every family photo.

I said we should tell someone, a guidance counselor maybe.

Edie's face hardened. "If you really think that'll do any good, you're even dumber than I thought."

I wasn't hurt, though, because again I had the peculiar feeling that I had something Edie wanted. That she looked at my life the way I'd once looked at her. As if proximity might be its own kind of transformation, as if she could briefly inhabit another world—the quiet rooms of my house, the rhythms unbroken from one day to the next. My mother in the kitchen counting out her calories. My father piling his loose change into little stacks on the counter.

For a long minute, we were silent. And then just like Edie said it would, the dark upstairs of her house burst into light. It started slow, a string of dynamite snaking room to room. But then the whole thing came alive, ablaze with light and shouting. The back door shot open, nearly knocked off its hinges. "Edie," Larry bellowed into the night.

I clutched at the ground beneath me, grass and dirt coming up in my palms. But Edie only laughed. Larry would pass out in an hour, she said, and she'd paint over the door in the morning. Everyone would pretend it never happened, and in a way it would be true. "Things are only ever bad for a minute," said Edie.

I tried to imagine what it would be like to live in Edie's house, its wild, murderous nights cleaved from its days. How things could happen in the dark, then disappear the next morning. But hard as I tried, I couldn't. My days moved stubbornly forward, one hinged to the next. I didn't understand my parents, occasionally raged against the sameness of their days, yet how utterly bereft I'd be, I thought now, to find the evidence of this sameness gone, to wake and find my father's little stacks of coins had vanished in the night.

A sound like a rocket came from behind us—a car gunning up the hill. It swung past our spot on the cliff, then arrowed up the road. Except that the road ended: beyond it, there were only trees, the cliff pitching sharply downward.

Edie and I looked at each other and ran. But as the road tapered off, we slowed, not meeting each other's gaze. Neither of us wanted to admit what we were seeing, which was the most strange and unspeakable kind of nothing: no car, no driver, no sound but the breath going in and out of our throats. I'd been listening for a crash, a stop—the screech of breaks or buckling of metal. But instead, there was only a fine bright dust rising all around us, and an unearthly quiet thrilled inside me. We'd trapdoored through a kind of sound barrier, dropped straight into the eye of darkness. I looked up.

But Edie was calling instead down into the trees. And then faintly, very faintly, a voice called back. "Please," it said. We started down the dark cliff, and the voice came closer. I thought how strange a thing for a body to say: *Please.* How strange a thing for a body to say when something terrible was about to befall it.

We reached the bottom of the hill, and what we saw made even Edie gasp. The car was at once vertical and upside-down, entirely suspended in the trees. It looked like something driven off a spectacular precipice in a movie, paused mid-scene. I tried to see through the cracked windshield, but there was only darkness. Then Edie pointed, and I saw a girl sitting on the ground below, like she'd just slid out.

Edie and I made our way toward her, car guts scattered all around. "Are you okay?" I asked.

The girl looked up at the car like she'd only now noticed. "Oh God."

"You probably shouldn't sit there," said Edie, and we helped her down to flat ground.

The girl seemed dazed yet somehow uninjured, only the most delicate of gashes on her leg. I thought I recognized her—a junior from high school, maybe—mysterious and a little bit famous, the way all teenagers looked to me. "Oh God," she kept saying each time she looked at the car.

"Maybe don't look over there," I suggested.

"Probably she has a concussion," said Edie.

The girl still had an arm around each of us, and it was hard to keep her vertical. Her head drooped like something not properly attached, and her nails clawed tiny moon marks in my neck. We spent a long while trying to ascertain her address, to no avail. "Do you guys want me to read your palms?" she asked.

"God no," said Edie.

"You"—the girl nodded drowsily in Edie's direction—"you're going to be famous."

"Yippee."

"But you've got a darkness too. I can see it all over your face."

Edie and I exchanged eyebrow messages.

I waited to hear my future, but the girl only nodded into the distance, then said in the manner of someone starting a ghost story, "Do you guys know about that rape that happened?"

We did know; everyone in school knew. But the strange part was, I couldn't remember who'd told me or even what they'd said. It was as if the story had been conveyed not in the usual way, person to person, but had existed quietly inside me and was only now revealed, some secret ore deeper than facts or words. I knew there were five boys, knew one of them was in our grade. Alex Baylor. The rest were older, high schoolers. I didn't know the girl, but somehow I could see her perfectly: her face turned to the side, cheek pressed to the ground, her eyes naked and wild. But I couldn't summon up the boys, not even Alex Baylor; they were only shadowy presences, hovering. What passed between these figures—the girl on the ground, the shadows floating up above—I couldn't begin to say, but the truth was, when I first heard, I'd thought: *It wouldn't be the worst thing*. It wasn't like you'd die, for instance. You could still get up and walk away. You wouldn't die if it happened.

Now I looked at the girl sitting between us, and a terrible thought occurred to me: it was her, the nameless girl, and now she'd plunged her car off the cliff. But instead she said: "It happened right here."

"No, it didn't," said Edie, who always knew more than I did. "It happened in the cornfield behind the Texaco."

The girl shrugged. "It's all the same fields around here."

Despite myself, I still wanted to hear my future. It wasn't so much that I thought the girl would know, just that I wanted to hear it spoken aloud: *One day, you will*. To be the subject of the sentence, launched by its glittering future tense into the dark unknown. Most of all, I wanted to be made legible, to hear this future self read back to me like a story. *You'll leave this town*, the girl might say. *You'll steal*

a car and drive all the way to California. You'll join a punk band and
give yourself a new name, something ruthless and beautiful.

Finally Edie and I decided to start walking. The girl, we hoped, would point us in the general direction of her house, and she tottered between us like a wobbly human Ouija. I looked back one last time. For the briefest of seconds, it seemed the car was no longer suspended but lifted as of a will all its own—a shoddy but nonetheless flying object, like something willed out of the past, out of all the days of waiting in the woods. It had come for us, finally, crashed through the hard physics of the possible—only it had come too late. Because what I wanted suddenly was to go back, to be whisked to the past which was also, somehow, the future—our real selves, our true selves, waiting in the trees. There was something back there, something I had to see. A faint echo still rang in my skull: *Please*, the voice said. *Please*.

On the first day of high school, I saw Edie at the other end of a long hallway. High school was jolting and sudden: too many bodies packed close together, pushed invisibly from room to room. I was being pulled in one direction and Edie another, but she turned back when I called her name. She did a quick shrug at me, then disappeared into the crowd.

After that, I didn't see her. I was in honors classes, and she'd been failing her regular classes since seventh grade. But still I expected to at least see her in passing. Maybe she'd dropped out, I thought. Maybe she'd moved. I walked by her house at night just in case I might catch a glimpse of her.

My favorite class was art. The art teacher, Mr. Doyle, spoke about forms and lines with a kind of reverence, a calm intensity. He took my drawings seriously, told me they were good but that I had to look closer: unsee the things too easily seen. In class, we broke this act of seeing into smaller and smaller pieces—the folds of a paper bag, the texture of wood grain. It was exhilarating: setting the world down piece by piece, watching it settle into forms and lines.

One day we started on circles. Mr. Doyle insisted the world was all circles, even things that appeared to be hard lines. There was a trick to it, a quickness of the hand, but I couldn't get mine to move right. All my circles came out lopsided, slow and overly studied.

I was in the midst of one of these circles when a scream pierced the quiet. All of us leapt from our desks to crowd around the door. We watched as two policemen emerged from the bathrooms by the gym, dragging a screaming body between them. Limbs kicked and flailed, and between the two dark police uniforms, the body seemed somehow to be flying, vaulted down the hall. At first, I thought it was a boy—his shaved head glinting in the light. But when the policemen came closer, the body thrashed to the side, and I saw it was Edie. Her head was shaved, her face gaunt, her bones clawing from her cheeks. But it was still her face, still the face I'd watched and dreamed of and studied, more familiar to me than my own. I could see the wildness of her eyes, the flash of her teeth. For a second, she was inches from me—so close I could've reached out and touched her. It felt like a rock kicked loose in my chest, an unbearable softness beneath.

"It's that druggie girl," someone observed.

I couldn't see Edie's face anymore. But she was still Edie, I told myself. Still Edie, screaming.

"All right." Mr. Doyle cleared his throat. "Let's get back to work, please."

I watched for a moment longer, then returned to my desk, to my page of failed circles. I sat very still and listened as Edie's screams grew quiet.

●

In the September of tenth grade, my mother died. It happened quickly: one day she couldn't get out of bed, and then she was diagnosed with pancreatic cancer. There was a round of experimental treatment, but she died the first week of September. I missed the first three weeks of school, and when I returned, I walked the halls like someone cut loose from gravity, hearing nothing and floating farther and farther away.

In those weeks, everything became about numbers: how many hours or days or Thursdays. How many days she was sick. I wrote down patterns, recurrences, though what all these numbers added up to, I couldn't say. I felt suspended at the edge of an unknown but fatal significance—some cosmic or earthly sum. I thought of Edie's pine needles, all her numbers and patterns, and wondered what it was she'd been counting to.

At school, death made you a kind of celebrity. Strangers felt license to talk to you or they went mute in your presence. Girls I didn't know told me about their grandmothers, their pets. I nodded as though I could hear them. I preferred the people who avoided me like I might be contagious, like death might infect them too.

And then there was Edie. She'd returned to school in my absence, to all remedial classes. She didn't go out of her way to speak to me, but when I cut Chemistry and slid in beside her at the picnic table outside, she acted as though I'd been sitting there all along. There were things I wanted to tell her, things I thought only she might understand. How silent my house had become and how betrayed I'd felt the morning my father put on his suit and tie and headed out the door. How I'd stopped eating and sleeping and how unearthly it felt to be unloosed from the world of human hungers. And most of all, how the very shapes of things had become slippery, nothing sure or solid. Was this how Edie had always felt? A kind of unsettling beneath her feet, the world too easily collapsed, not even the walls of the body certain.

Edie was sitting atop the picnic table wielding a pen like a knife, carving something indecipherable into the wood—a secret treatise, I thought, a code. A map that might usher me into this new, formless world.

Lately, I no longer wanted to draw things, but after years of absence, the words of my childhood had returned, the universe teetering faint and queasy in my skull. Only now these spells came on unprompted, shadowing suddenly out of my brain, and the words themselves had become indecipherable. They loomed huge and dark in my head.

For the briefest of seconds, I wondered if these were the words Edie was writing, words made finally legible on the picnic table. But when I looked closer, I saw they were only lyrics: *This is what you'll get, this is what you'll get—*

"You're back," was all Edie said, as though I'd just been gone a moment.

I shrugged. "I guess so."

I wanted to say something else, but right then a tall boy strode across the courtyard and sat down on the picnic table, folding up his long limbs on the other side of Edie. When I looked at him, I felt myself sliding toward something—a sharp turn or a stomach-shuddering drop. He was beautiful in the way of things at once strange and familiar, or maybe this was just how it seemed to me. He had a face that refused to stick, something blurry about it. Like a smudge at the corner of your eye, too close to see. You always had to look again.

"Do you know Damien?" Edie asked me.

I didn't. I guessed he was a senior. And yet he insisted he knew me, that we'd ridden the bus together long ago. I tried to summon him up, a faceless figure drifting in the bus's backseat, and listened as he described me as I had been: a small girl hunched with too many books, quiet and dreamy. The longer he talked, the more he seemed to lengthen like a shadow in my brain, a kind of echo rippling outward across time. Maybe I had known him. Maybe I had.

The next day, I was surprised to find Edie at my locker. I never saw her in the hallway, never saw her in the building at all. She seemed to exist at school only outside at the picnic tables. Now she was asking if I wanted to come to a party. "Well, not really a party," she appended. "More like a get-together at Dave's house."

I didn't know who Dave was, but a glittery feeling passed over my skin. Because I knew Edie would never invite me, knew it wasn't her asking. Yes, I nodded, turning away to hide my smile. Yes, I'd go.

"Parties," my father murmured as if from far away. "Good, good. That's what you should be doing at this age."

At dusk, a car appeared outside, Edie smoking in the passenger seat. I'd never seen the driver before, but when I climbed into the back, I saw he was holding Edie's hand. *Oh*, I thought. He was Steve, said Edie. Damien sat in the back beside me.

It was October already, night coming sooner. Cold air flooded my face, and Edie's cigarette embers streaked past like meteors. I'd never been in a car that wasn't driven by someone's parent. But then, I remembered, I'd also never been alive in a month my mother hadn't.

I thought how strange it was to find Edie again, Edie who was quieter, her face blank, like her real face was being held captive behind it. Edie who was someone I did and didn't recognize as the car hurtled toward the freeway. Bass from the radio trembled inside my chest. My hair flew wild as flames around my head. The feeling speeding down the ramp onto the freeway was like being plunged into the weightless shock of space.

Dave's house was an old farmhouse, peeled paint like broken ribs. Its insides hit me like a wall of smoke: hazy limbs everywhere, tapestries billowing loosely from walls. Somebody somewhere strumming a guitar.

"Annie," called a gray-bearded man. He emerged out of the haze as if to embrace me, and I stepped back, alarmed.

"Dave calls all girls Annie," Edie told me, as though this explained it. In the car, I'd learned that Dave was an old hippie who'd lost his license, and Edie and Steve sometimes ferried him on errands around town.

"Annie like Anna," nodded Dave. "It goes forwards, it goes backwards. You see?" He'd known a girl named Anna once, he said. Or maybe it was Annabel—it was a long time ago, in Tennessee. People believed all kinds of things in the South, he went on, though he himself wasn't a believer, just a great pretender, which was sometimes the same thing. I couldn't quite follow how he got from one thing to the next, but I nodded along. "People'd think I was some kind of prophet," he concluded. "Which I'm not."

All the people around us seemed to be nodding too, as though to distant music. When someone handed me a joint, I pretended to inhale, but even this made me feel loopy and sick.

I realized I didn't know where Edie was when Damien motioned to the door. "Want to go outside?"

I glanced around for Edie. I wanted to tell her where I was going. But she'd vanished into the crowd.

Outside, Damien and I walked across the field toward a dark line of trees. For a while, my limbs felt loose and disjointed, but then I forgot them, forgot myself, and anyway, Damien seemed already to know everything about me. He knew my father's name and where he worked. He knew about my mother. He knew how I'd stopped eating, how I kept dreaming of something deathly and radioactive in the refrigerator—how when I woke, I had to steal through the dark house to see if it was true. He knew, somehow, about the words in my head, as though he could read every unreadable thing in me, too.

Talking to him was like moving through a dream world: everything known by unknown means, and only when you stopped to think about it did any of it seem awry. When I asked why I'd never seen him all this time, he told me he'd been in military school for a while and then on the run, crossing the country on trains. He could hack into computers, any computer, and he'd hacked into the wrong one. The FBI had come looking for him. He mentioned names I knew and names I didn't: Russian mobsters, a meth dealer named Jesus, Heinrich Himmler. A man who lived at the edge of town and set fire to houses. Who set fires just because he could.

As Damien spoke, I felt the ground shift beneath me, the world made and unmade: the cold mud beneath my sneakers, my own thoughts. It was terrifying and also beautiful to be known: every thought, every secret. I pictured my insides like a house broken into, a computer cracked open. All my insides flung out onto the lawn. All the scattered little pieces of me held up to the light. I thought of the phrase Ms. Green had taught us in English the year before: *suspension of disbelief.* This was how I felt now: suspended. When my mother died, I'd entered into a world where anything could happen, and who was I to say what it could or couldn't do to you.

There was a horn honking in the distance, then Edie shouting through the trees: "Stop fucking, you two. It's time to go."

Then we were in the car again. We pulled up in front of my house, where Damien insisted on walking me to the door. He paused there for a moment, and when he spoke, he seemed to be speaking not to me, exactly, but to an emptiness just above my head: "You're so beautiful."

Afterward, I stood in the doorway, watching the car disappear down the street. I felt as I had some nights returning from the woods long ago, nights so huge they held inside them entire eras. There would be a moment just as I stepped through the door when I was not yet inside—the clamor of the woods still churning in my chest, dreamy indoor sounds tugging at me weakly—and for a minute, I'd stand there, knowing there was no way of ever telling who I was or who I'd become.

"He lies," Edie told me one day, appearing a second and final time at my locker.

"Lies how?" I asked, though I'd already made up my mind not to believe her. She didn't want to warn me; what she wanted was to take something, the way she always had. *You're just jealous*, I thought. *You're jealous because we're in love.*

Edie's eyes flashed. For a minute, she was the old Edie, the Edie I'd glimpsed through the classroom door. It was like witnessing the pale aftermath of a meteor flown by—something cosmic and gone, particles trailing in its wake. And even as I tried to summon my most unyielding stare, I knew there was still a part of me that would give Edie anything—my tooth, my voice, all the stopped-up words in my throat. I'd give it up, give everything away, if only she promised to take me with her.

But she wouldn't. Standing there at my locker, I knew she was offering me something—not the thing I wanted but *something*—reaching across some unfathomable breach. I understood all this, all that hovered in the silence between us. Or I thought I did.

Edie was the first to look away. "He lies. That's all."

Later that day, I followed Damien down to the train tracks behind school. I hadn't even known the tracks were there, but I saw now that the trains had been running back and forth all this time, ferrying their long cargo just past the trees. I remembered the time Edie and I found the river out in the woods, the river which was barely a creek. But it stunned us nonetheless: the flash of silver through the trees, the rush of water, and how something could be there all along, running invisibly.

"What class are you cutting?" I asked Damien. I'd known him less than two weeks, but already I'd discovered how easy it was to simply stop going.

"Actually," said Damien, "I'm sort of suspended." He hadn't wanted to tell me, he said, since I was part of the reason. He'd gotten into a fight with John Bierbauer, who'd called me "that Jew girl."

"Oh," I said, not knowing what to feel. I didn't believe him. I did.

Damien looked at me. Maybe I was supposed to say thank you now, I thought. Maybe that was what you did when someone defended your honor.

"I need to do something," said Damien. He closed his eyes, and his mouth, I realized, was careening toward mine, unstoppable as a comet. Before I knew what I was doing, I jerked away, his lips landing somewhere in my hair.

"I'm sorry," I said. "I'm so sorry." I ran all the way back to school.

I found Edie atop the picnic table, still carving. All at once, I wanted to tell her about the botched kiss. All at once, I didn't.

"Where's Damien?" she asked, not looking up.

I was surprised: she knew everything before I did. "He got suspended."

"Yeah," she scoffed. "Like five years ago."

I looked at her, not understanding. "What do you mean?"

But Edie stared only at the picnic table, at the words she was carving. Whatever possible world had opened between us at my locker was gone now, her face hard and closed.

"What do you mean?" I asked again.

Edie looked at me finally, rolled her eyes.

It was night, Edie and I waiting in the car, the gas station a glowing orb in the dark—the only bright thing for miles. Inside it, we could see Steve and Damien at the counter, each with a six-pack in their hands. They were talking—probably about me, I thought, about how I couldn't even kiss. At last, I couldn't take it anymore. I told Edie what had happened.

She stared out into the dark, silent as an oracle. I stared at the back of her head. "So he kissed you," she said finally, "and you didn't let him?"

"It just surprised me," I said. It would be worse to admit I'd never kissed anyone. "I just didn't know that was what was happening."

"What did you think you were doing out there?" she said, meaning the woods, the train tracks.

I was silent. Even I knew the worst thing you could be was a tease.

"Well," Edie said, still staring into the dark, "now you have to let him kiss you." This she pronounced not as advice or suggestion but like something she'd read somewhere, a future already certain.

An emptiness plummeted inside my chest. It wasn't what I'd wanted her to say. Worse, it didn't sound like her. It was like one of her grown-up phrases from long ago. *That's the way it goes.* What I'd wanted was for Edie to turn around, look me in the eye—to say one true thing, though I didn't know what that thing might be.

"What time is it?" she asked finally.

"I don't know," I said.

Because there was only the dark, the low pulse of night, and then Steve and Damien sliding into the seats beside us. We drove down streets I didn't recognize, and when I felt the tires slipping over gravel, the car nosing down the side of the road, I thought for a moment it was giving out beneath us. But then I saw Steve's hands moving slow and deliberate on the wheel, and I understood that we were turning, high beams flooding the field. The lights ticked out, and we moved through a darkness that seemed to be vibrating, gathering—cornstalks shuddering stiffly against metal. The field was high and all around us, and I didn't know where we were going, only that I'd been there before.

CHOREOGRAPH

My stepsister is writing a choreography. It's the choreography of her voices, the ones that speak to her at all hours of the day. They're loudest in the morning, she says, when they cut like light. You ask her a question and she repeats the words back, but slower. It's hard to hear over the din.

How do you write a choreography? Historically, this has been hard to say. If you had dancers, you could tell them how to move. You could position and reposition their arms and legs. But say you have no dancers. Say you have only voices. What is the notation? For centuries, there were attempts to create a musical score of the torso and limbs. Notators of the body's rise and fall through gravity. We have their notes, their scribblings—the things crossed out, crossed out again. The transcription remains difficult.

My stepsister is reading the diary of Vaslav Nijinsky, the famous dancer. What she loves most, she says, is the way he invented his own lexicon. It began in Budapest, where he was detained during the First World War. His choreographic notes had been mistaken for sabotage, secret codes and ciphers. In a way, it was true: Nijinsky was sketching out the terms of a private language, one he hoped would transport his dances—and maybe himself—across space and time.

The problem with dance, my stepsister tells me, is that it's susceptible to vanishing. Stuck in the body, the most transient of medi-
ums, it flickers, then disappears. Maybe Nijinsky understood this
and wanted to make a record. Or maybe he sensed that his life was
already pointed toward a kind of erasure. Within a few years of their
creation, most of Nijinsky's choreographies were lost. Decades later,
the most famous was pieced back together from fragments. Nijinsky
himself went mad.

For as long as I've known her, my stepsister has been a dancer of one
kind or another. Even after she started hearing voices, she danced
off and on as an understudy in New York. And maybe this is why, at
twenty-two, I found myself in Brooklyn, a research assistant at the
small local newspaper where I'd eventually become a writer. New
York, it seemed, was a quickening in my stepsister, and I wanted to
be pulled by its current too.

What I write about now is buildings—their peculiar accumulations
of people and history across the years. When I was assigned this particular column, I knew nothing about architecture, nothing about
buildings except for having spent most of my life living in them.
Now I leaf through old floor plans in archives. I walk the city looking for the odd cracks where history shows through. "Building Stories" is what my column is called, though I didn't call it that. What
I've learned writing these stories is that history only looks heavy and
solid. In fact, it won't ever stay still.

For a while, my stepsister talked about setting down a dance floor in
her room, which was the attic of my father and stepmother's house.
I was fifteen that year and I'd recently run away. I'd run away, then
come to live with my father. My stepsister, meanwhile, had dropped

out of college in New York, and she'd returned to this house, too. No one talked about why either of us were there, least of all her or me. Instead, I lay awake at night listening to her pacing in the attic. I stared at the ceiling and imagined I could chart the trajectory of her footsteps, decode the impossible things they were trying to say.

My stepsister's choreography will contain not only her voices but the voices of all the people she's met in hospitals, all the staff and patients, all the residents of the halfway house where she now lives. Some days, my stepsister tells me, the gravity becomes loose there. It's like she's floating in a strange land. There's a man in the halfway house who also has problems with gravity. They're long and elaborate problems with complicated physics, but in short, he believes that gravity has weakened all around him. He wears several layers of clothing and a backpack weighted down with rocks. No one is allowed to say the word *go* to him, lest he rise up and float away.

The halfway house is three hours away, in a small town where buses don't go. I have to rent a car and drive through upstate New York. But this is still better than it used to be, because for years my stepsister was in and out of hospitals and didn't want to be seen at all. The halfway house is the first place she's lived where I can come visit her. When I'm there, we walk together through the little town—past the Salvation Army, the post office, the train tracks—trying to talk across the distance. Does she remember the time we did this or that, I sometimes ask. "No," she most often says. "I have a hard time remembering."

My stepsister tells me she's fallen in love with a musician. Or she's fallen in love with his voice. He sings through her speakers, she says, and it's like he's right there in the room beside her. She tells me this back at the halfway house, silhouetted against her bright window. A few weeks before, she drove all the way to the town where the musician lives, and for a week, she rode around searching for him in the streets. "I think I scared him," she says, and then shrugs—this is beside the point. She shows me the stack of letters she's written, all marked *Refused*.

I think: Would I, could I, drive to a far-off town just to chase the sound of someone's voice?

Yes, I think. No.

Then: I've been doing it all my life.

For a while, I became a student of voices. The year I was twenty, I went to Banaras, India. Every Thursday for a year, I took a rickshaw across the city to the tomb of Bahadur Shahid, a Sufi saint. Thursday was the day women crowded onto the tomb grounds. They unbraided their hair and rocked back and forth—slowly at first, then faster. A dance with the unsayable. When they spoke, they spoke in many voices but never as themselves—never as women, but as ghosts; male ghosts, mostly, with deep voices. *Bhut-pret*, they called them. Ghost-spirits. In Banaras, these were often the same thing.

I went to Banaras to follow a boy. He'd won a prestigious fellowship to study at the city university, and though it should have been clear that our relationship was near its end, I decided to go along with him—our lives, I thought, would be different on the other side of the world, shaken from their ruts and patterns. But I also had a secret reason for wanting to go to Banaras, one I barely admitted to myself. I'd read about the tomb of Bahadur Shahid, about the women speaking in voices—how they traveled great distances and how they left

changed, their ghosts at least temporarily assuaged. In some far corner of my mind, I thought I might solve the puzzle of my stepsister's
voices; I thought I might save her.

Sometimes women at the tomb spun so quickly, they fainted. Or
they hurled their bodies away from something invisible, as if to see
how far they could go—how far the body could be flung and still
return intact. Temple laymen on the loudspeaker pestered for dona-
tions. Beggars at the gate called out for alms. The whole place was
dizzy with noise, the smell of marigolds rotting in the heat. In the
shade sat husbands, sisters, wide-eyed children. They watched as possessed women fell in and out of the light.

"Social constructions of madness" was what I told people my senior
thesis was about, although as usual, we don't know why we go the
places we do. We don't know whose voice we speak in.

My stepsister at twelve had long black hair, an easy laugh, a Morton's
toe. She had a song-and-dance routine she did in the living room, an
elaborate system of call-and-responses. We were all her audience, her
chorus, her backup singers. The day I met her, when I was four, she
sang a song that began: "There once was a little unamoo." What was
an unamoo? I never knew exactly. She was full of words like that—
words I knew, but only when she spoke them. A private language
that existed all around her. Meanwhile, I watched. I whispered. I
wore her hand-me-downs like shrouds. I studied each and every one
of her gestures and pulled on my second toe—it would grow longer,
I thought, like hers—and this pulling became its own gesture, a secret sign between us. I was her mimic, her mime. I wanted to make
myself a double. Or I wanted to grow inward, truer—toward the
unspeakable part of me she seemed to speak.

There are the usual ways of falling in love. Less talked about are the ways in which one person may decide to become another. To transform, to transfigure. To come through the slow sludge of metamorphosis and find oneself changed.

"This is my little sister," she used to say, introducing me. No one else in our family talked this way. Always we were stepdaughters. Stepmothers and stepfathers. We made no claims on each other. But when she said it—*my little sister*—people would look at us and say, "Oh yes, I see it. You look so alike." Although, of course, we looked nothing alike. *This is my little sister.* I wanted to believe her, to belong to the sort of correspondence that could be traced between our faces. To see, inscribed in flesh, the invisible knots between us. And when she said it, I did. She was that rare sort of person who could make you see what wasn't there.

Now, years later, at the halfway house, we meet a shuffling man in the hall. She links her arm through mine. "This is my little sister," she says.

"Oh yes," says the shuffling man, blinking. "Yes, I see it."

She looks at me and I look back. Our oldest trick.

"What do the voices say?" I ask. I've mostly forgotten the words we used to speak. *Didy* for *tiny. Deep* for *sleep.* They belong to another time and place, a parallel universe of my stepsister's invention. She thinks for a minute, weighing how much to tell me. "Sometimes they say they're never going away, even after I die. Sometimes they're just sort of silly. They call me a little unamoo."

In New York, I go to the library in Midtown, its catacombs of pneumatic tubes stirring beneath. I find the memoir of Nijinsky's younger sister, Bronislava Nijinska—like Nijinsky, a dancer with the Ballets Russes. Together with Bronislava, Nijinsky began choreographing his most famous dance, *The Afternoon of a Faun*, in secret. All throughout their rehearsals, Nijinsky had his sister dance his own part, that of the faun. He worked, Bronislava wrote in her diary, like a sculptor, positioning and repositioning her arms and legs. *I am like a piece of clay that he is molding, shaping into each pose and change of movement.* He wanted her to move not *to* but rather *through* the music, to come crashing through any semblance of tempo or time. The *Faun* would be a dance with no dance steps in it; it would be a new kind of movement—a kind of movement that cut. It would strip each gesture down to something raw and elemental, betray it as a thing of bone and blood.

When they were children, the Nijinsky siblings' older brother fell from a fourth-floor window, suffering brain injury and spending the rest of his life in an asylum in Russia. Nijinsky would visit him in the psychiatric ward, which also housed neurological patients—dystonia, epilepsy, cerebral palsy. Later, Nijinsky's choreographies would come to be known for their spasm-like quality, their proclivity for almost pathological contortion. During the premiere of *The Rite of Spring*, danced to Stravinsky's then-incendiary score, audience members reportedly shouted, "Call a doctor!" Nijinsky wrote: *I like lunatics because I know how to talk to them. When my brother was in a lunatic asylum, I loved him and he felt me.... I understood the life of a lunatic.*

At eight, I sat drawing on the attic stairs while my stepsister's footsteps orbited above. She was always moving through the attic—laughing into the phone, flipping through cassette tapes, tacking more and more things to the walls. Often it was enough, just sitting on the attic stairs. Like I had to eddy at the edges of her. The rest of the house felt stuck and silent, but the attic was full of movement, sound. Music trembled in the walls—a chorus of trapped bees. Galaxies of dust spun in the light. To me, the attic was huge and unfathomably dense with things: posters, paints, a neon EXIT sign, stacks and stacks of *Bazaar* magazines, tiny vials of beads. My stepsister was always arranging these things, arranging and rearranging. I'd run my fingers over them one by one.

My favorite thing in the attic was the seashell. My stepsister's father was Japanese, and when I was six she went to Okayama to visit family. She brought back a seashell with a tiny painting inside: two women looking out into the distance. "That's you and that's me," I told her, opening the shell and then closing it again.

Sometimes I conscripted her into a game in which all the attic was water and her mattress was the only raft at sea. I watched as the water rose higher and higher. She saved me every time.

A drawing I made of the attic at eight shows a watery and underground room, full of unknowable things. Not a literal depiction, but a kind of catacombs—inspired, mostly, by the witch's lair in *Snow White*. It too was filled with mysterious objects: relics, bones. Things dense with transformation. A subterranean river ran through it. This was the sort of place I drew: dark shadows, arcane objects, a river. Neither my stepsister nor I were depicted; the attic seemed to hover in dreamtime, someone looking in, floating outside.

Blood is thicker than water. This is what my father liked to say. "Like you and your stepsister," he said one day in the car when I was nine. "She's my stepdaughter, but you're my daughter. I can love her, but it's not the same." He wasn't really talking about her, I knew. He was talking about my mother and stepfather, my other family. He was staking a claim to me. He was talking about blood—flesh and blood, ties of blood—but it was the water I kept thinking about. "Do you understand?" my father asked.

I nodded, but really I thought about my stepsister. I thought: *I must be a girl made of water.* Because I loved her most of all.

Some days, I find myself pulled toward a particular corner of the city—a street, a building, a block—and I think of the instructions I read once in the Vedas: how in the forest, the devotee must choose a tree "on the farther side of the nearer" and "on the nearer side of the farther." And yet, the Vedas also insist, this tree is never random. No one has ever been able to make much sense of the Vedas—all their riddling instructions, all those elaborate gestures to be performed and performed again. Or maybe this is what a gesture is: a kind of language trapped beneath the skin.

The December I was fifteen, I ran away with an older boy I barely knew and wound up in the attic of a near-condemned house. The attic was empty save for a bare mattress shot through with cigarette burns, and for three days and nights, I lay there very still, floating in a kind of dreamtime. Did I think about my stepsister's attic? Later, when I tried to arrange those days into something like order, I some-times thought of this as a period of waiting: waiting to be found, to be saved. But at the time it didn't feel that way. At the time, I didn't believe there was anything to wait for. The future had dropped off like a cliff, and I lay floating in an infinite present.

When I arrived at my father's house, it was early in the morning and I hadn't slept in days. Out on the sidewalk, my breath rose up like ragged ghosts. Purple-yellow sky swelled like a bruise. I lay down on my father's couch and fell asleep, and when I woke, it was to the sound of my stepsister's voice. Sun was slanting through the blinds, and she sat perched beside me, pushing the hair out of my eyes. "Somebody's deepy," she said, then pulled on my second toe.

In those days, the smallest of details became fraught with meaning: the number of hours, the number of days. Walking to school, I looked at houses and heard them whispering secrets. I saw messages in the sidewalk cracks. I felt not right in time—everything was a backward premonition or déjà vu for a future yet to come. Out of nowhere, I sometimes felt invisible fists knuckling through my limbs, my jaw. Ghost fists, I called them—quick and numbing. There's nothing like a fist—even a disembodied one—to unsay every word in your head.

One day at the tomb, a young woman in a green sari writhed on the ground while relatives crouched around her, asking: "What do you want?" Later, someone told me the woman was possessed by a long-dead uncle-in-law, a man she'd never met. "What do you want?" the relatives asked in deferential tones, and the woman answered in the grammatical masculine. But in a moment of her writhing, she made a sudden movement and her sari came loose; then she was a woman again. "Cover her," someone said quickly. "Cover her."

Men, too, came to the tomb, though they were fewer. One lay catatonic, his arm raised and rigid in the air. Another stood at the gate singing Bollywood songs—movie stars had taken up residence inside his head. But mostly, the men at the tomb were husbands watching their wives fall in and out of trance. Ghosts preferred to enter women, one husband told me. Ghosts were afraid of men. People were always telling me things about ghosts. At night, I made lists. *Ghosts died bad deaths. Ghosts hide in braids. Ghosts prowl around near cre-*

mation grounds, lone trees, dropped coins at the fair. Ghosts are afraid. Ghosts lurk in stomach acid, in wounds. Ghosts come upon you suddenly when you walk out of your house.

What do the voices say? My stepsister doesn't tell me the worst things. As usual, she's protecting me. Lately, she's been working on an art project in which she hands out little painted cards to strangers around town. Each one has a message. The one she gives me says *S.E.A.R.C.H.* Others, she pushes out of sight. I catch a glimpse of one that says *Please don't hurt me.*

Ghosts prefer to enter women. By which was meant, also, that women's bodies were easily possessed. At the tomb, women cried out in pain or contorted noiselessly on the ground. All around there was the sound of sobbing. I would like to say that I felt something—a kind of transcription of the invisible, maybe. Ghost into flesh, body into sound. But mostly I felt queasy with the spinning and the heat, a feeling like hurtling even when I sat very still, my spine pressed up against the stone wall. I ran my fingers along the ridges in the ground as if to tell myself: you are here.

For Nijinsky, madness was also a kind of muteness. After the age of twenty-nine, he rarely spoke. He did leave a diary: a six-week outpouring of words. At the time, he was being seen by a local doctor who administered frequent word association tests. But Nijinsky seems to have turned this associativeness inward, his connections mounting feverishly across the page, alighting on everything and sticking to nothing. They multiplied too quickly for language to bear. Or perhaps Nijinsky knew he might never speak again and didn't have time to bother with semantics. Already his wife, troubled by her husband's erratic behavior, wanted him to see a psychiatrist in Zurich.

As it happened, the psychiatrist was Eugen Bleuler, the man who'd recently coined the term "schizophrenia." Before Bleuler, people had been mad, hysterical, criminally insane. Never before had someone been schizophrenic. Nijinsky suspected—rightly, it turned out—that he might never return from Zurich. And so he sat upstairs and recorded the sounds of the house all around him: footsteps, shut doors, hushed voices on the telephone. He felt madness rolling in like a tide. He wrote: *The audience started laughing. I started laughing. I laughed in my dance. The audience too laughed in the dance. The audience understood my dances, for they wanted to dance too...I wanted to dance more, but God said to me, "Enough." I stopped.*

I ran away many times as a teenager, but only once did I make it to New York. It was December again, but now I was sixteen. A whole year had passed since I found myself in the attic. I took the train in from New Jersey, the long, dark tunnel shuttling me beneath the river. Then the pressure of the darkness changed and I felt the density of the city rolling up above. I made my way up the stairs into its light. On the corner of Seventh Avenue, I stood terrified: around every corner, a mugger, a murderer, a policeman waiting to cart me back home. But I also felt alive, made new, because I was now a tiny atom of the chaos all around me, a riot of voices and sounds. The street took my heart and skipped it, and I felt blown wide open—so wide that I could feel inside me the entire city, opening and closing across the years.

I made my way up Eighth Avenue to Port Authority. There, I waited in the dark, then boarded a bus bound for the other side of the country. And as I did, I felt for the first time that I was writing myself into the story of my life. That this was the first true thing I'd ever written.

Nijinsky's last performance was an improvised one in a hotel in St. Moritz in 1919. After being detained in Budapest, he managed to escape to Vienna, then to neutral Switzerland. Some two hundred people waited for him in the lobby. But instead of dancing, Nijinsky sat on the stage and stared at the crowd in silence for close to half an hour. Then he launched into a long tirade, admonishing the audience for failing to stop the war. "Now I will dance you the war, with its suffering, with its destruction, with its death," he said. "The war which you did not prevent." Finally, he started to dance, but just as quickly stopped. This was also the day he started his diary.

The year I was fifteen was the start of one war, and then another—Afghanistan, Iraq. I kept dreaming about a bomb shelter, where I sat huddled with women whose language I couldn't speak. Bombs fell above us and our ears bled from the noise. My stepsister, meanwhile, paced in front of the evening news, looking into the distance at something the rest of us couldn't see. Sometimes she spent whole days and nights pacing, wandering in circles, moving through the house like a leaf drifting downstream. Eventually she'd wind up in the living room, where the rest of us sat, TV jabbering, not knowing what to do. Once, she stopped mid-step and gasped in terror. She stood so close to me, I could've reached out and touched her, could've tried to pull her back into the world of visible things. But I didn't. I couldn't move. This is the thing about terror—yours or someone else's. It lifts you up and out of your skin. It scatters the pieces of you.

One afternoon, my stepsister sat down on the couch and didn't move or speak for days, her hair a dark flame matting above her head. The day my father and stepmother told me they were taking her to the hospital, I ran upstairs and covered my ears, afraid to hear the screaming. But I heard nothing, just the sound of the front door opening and closing. I went to the window and watched, shocked by how easy it all was—how my father and stepmother walked with my stepsister between them, each with a hand on her elbow, and how quietly she simply went.

But I'd also written this already. When I was thirteen, I'd had to write an essay for school. We were supposed to write about a person—any person—but of course the only person I could think of writing about was her. This was always how it seemed when it came to my stepsister. Like I'd chosen her, but also like there was never any choice—my tree on the nearer side of the farther. I don't remember what I wrote except for the last few pages, in which I did something I'd never done before: I wrote an ending that hadn't really happened. And yet, somehow, it felt truer. In the last scene, my stepsister was in the hospital—perhaps, it was implied, after trying to kill herself. Meanwhile, alone in my father's house, I ventured up the attic stairs. I lay down on her bed, which then somehow transformed into a hospital bed. I looked out the window, and my stepsister and I were both, for a second, seeing the exact same thing.

What compelled me to write this? Likely, I was reading a lot of Sylvia Plath at the time. A week after I turned in the essay, my father called. My stepsister had jumped out of a moving car into traffic—her first suicide attempt. I was at my mother's house, and his voice got farther and farther away. The floor rose up at me as I sat down, stunned, like I'd just plummeted from some great distance.

At thirteen, the essay was proof, tangible evidence of the quasi-mystical connection between us. Of course, in retrospect, my stepsister had already said the word *hospital* one night at dinner, and I'd watched as everyone looked away. In that silence, I'd understood everything, even if I didn't know it yet. Still, after my father's phone call, I ripped graph paper out of my math notebook and drew the first of many diagrams on my bedroom floor. I wanted to turn myself into a diagram—to become a line, a vector moving through space and time—and to understand how my stepsister's vector intersected with mine. But in the end it looked less like a graph and more like a star chart—a mad scribble of vague constellations and convergences. Things connected mostly by belief.

The day Nijinsky was diagnosed as schizophrenic, he went back to his Zurich hotel room and locked himself in. After twenty-four hours, his wife called the police, who broke down the door, and he was committed to a psychiatric ward. Later, when Nijinsky's sister visited, she found her brother walled deep inside his own silence. He hadn't spoken in months. He had the peculiar stare of catatonics, as though he were peering out beyond the edge of time. Bronislava talked to him about her own work—her students, her dancing—but Nijinsky appeared not to hear. Finally, she told him she had devised two ballets, and he looked straight at her. "The *ballet* is never devised," he said. "The *ballet* must be created." Then he looked away.

There were years my stepsister barely spoke at all. I began to feel she was gone in some irrevocable way, that I might never meet her again, not really. I was living in Brooklyn by then, and she would often ride the train into the city to take dance classes. It was hard to keep in touch with her—she never answered her phone—but the few times I managed to track her down, we met and wandered silently through the streets. For a while, I'd try to fill this silence with words, but it was like making conversation with a ghost: inevitably, you grow suspicious of your own voice. Inevitably, you start to think it's you who can't help addressing invisible people on the street. Once we walked and walked until we ran out of sidewalk and wound up in an empty playground at the Chelsea Piers. My stepsister went around touching things: the plastic joints and junctures, the *x*'s and *o*'s of a giant tic-tac-toe. I followed as though in a trance. In my dreams I was always following her like this—through cornfields, through houses, up and down stairs. I could never seem to catch up. At the playground's gate, my stepsister said the first words she'd said in hours: "I have to go."

I said I'd walk her back to Midtown, but she shook her head. For a second I feared I'd misunderstood—that she didn't just mean she had to go from this pier, this city, but that she had to leave in some bigger, more nebulous way. "I have to be by myself," she said finally, and I watched as she grew smaller in the distance.

But even in the years we didn't speak, sometimes a gesture of hers would find me. I'd be crossing a street and pull my sleeves down over my hands in the exact way she used to. This was the sort of thing I remembered most in her absence. Something speechless and alive— a certain expression, a movement of the hand. The language of the body breaking through.

At fifteen, I also went for long periods without speaking. I hid in the library during lunch and cut the classes in which I knew I'd be forced to talk. I suppose I should say that it was something to be overcome, a step on some long arc of redemption. But in truth, it felt wild, freeing—to ask and be asked nothing; to forget my tongue, my name. To see that speechlessness was everywhere, all around me, not the exception but the rule: every object I touched a kind of unspeaking portal, a way through.

My stepsister was hospitalized three times that year. I was never allowed to visit. I pictured endless white hallways, my stepsister slowly erased inside them. Each time she came back, it was like her memory had been shaken loose of its contents—a common side effect of electroconvulsive therapy. I began to think our shared language would disappear, all our memories, that I would have to become the guardian of these things.

After school, while my father and stepmother were at the hospital, I'd climb up to the attic, ready to fly down the stairs at any moment, as though I were doing something illicit. I tried on her clothes and sometimes stole them: a T-shirt, a necklace. Like I'd once done as a child, I walked around the attic and touched her possessions one by one—a ghost trying to remember the world of things.

The earth is the head of God, wrote Nijinsky. *God is fire in the head. I am alive as long as I have a fire in my head. My pulse is an earthquake. I am an earthquake.*

In his diary, Nijinsky made grand pronouncements and plans. He wrote in the voice of God. He would build a bridge across the Atlantic Ocean. He would reverse the Earth's extinction and create a new kind of fountain pen—to be called "God." *I am a man in a trance*, he wrote. *I can write in a trance. I am in a trance of God.*

But there had always been a certain blurring of the lines when it came to Nijinsky—his very existence seemed to spur metaphysical speculation. People claimed he'd learned to levitate. He'd studied yogic tricks to unloosen his limbs from gravity—there could be no other explanation for the way he flew across the stage. Nijinsky himself spoke of being able to descend more slowly than ascend, of pausing mid-leap. It was as though, in those moments, he'd come unloosed from time. He could watch from somewhere outside his body, he said, as he glided through the air.

On the day he was taken to the hospital, Nijinsky reportedly said to his wife, "Little wife, you are bringing my death warrant." He lived the rest of his life in and out of institutions, undergoing hundreds of treatments and procedures—among them, an experimental insulin treatment, which shocked the body into a coma. Some called his diary a very long suicide note.

My stepsister jumped out of moving cars. She overdosed on pills. I lost count of the number of times. Often I could remember these attempts only by which apartment I was living in. They formed a constellation across the city: Bensonhurst, Gowanus, East Harlem. Once, after my stepsister swallowed a bottle of Tylenol, they had to attach her to an artificial liver machine for days. I was in Harlem then. It was snowing. She shouldn't have lived, the doctor said.

Each time, my stepmother cried for weeks. Each time, I looked out at the city and felt that my stepsister was trapped—someone neither here nor there, someone always pointed toward an exit. And sometimes, on the worst days, a ghost of a voice whispered in my ear. *Go*, I'd think. *If that's what you want, just go.*

In Hindi, the word for tomb, *samadhi*, is also a yogic term associated with asceticism. A sadhu may "take samadhi," crawling into his own tomb and lying very still for days. But it's also said that during this time, the sadhu may still be seen hovering around other parts of the city, granting miracles. The figure of the Pir, someone who has died a violent or spectacular death and become a kind of deity, is sometimes associated with the entombed holy man—the Pir's violent end conflated with the suffering of the ascetic. Both lie there in their tombs, breathing very little. Both are said to be awake.

There are years that disappear from your life almost entirely. Minutes that rip the skin off time. After I came to my father's, I forgot the three days and nights, the mattress in the attic. The form of this forgetting changed and kept changing. At first it was a kind of willed oblivion, a spell I could trick myself into. Then it was only blankness, a shape that refused to fall down into language. And then one day it did. It was during a game of Never Have I Ever—a game people played primarily to find out who'd had sex. I'd been dragged to a party by my neighbor, a Russian girl who, like me, had been plunked down into our high school in the middle of freshman year. Afterward, she whispered, "Who did you have sex with?"

So I told her. I don't know what I said exactly. I didn't think I was saying anything remarkable. But whatever it was must have alarmed her. Her eyes grew very wide, and in her accent, the word sounded like *rip*. "That's rip," she said, and for a second, I looked at her, stunned. That was the word, the secret word I'd felt.

I don't know what to say, Nijinsky wrote. *I don't know what to silence.* In Budapest, while under house arrest, he began devising the *Faun's* notation in earnest. He was trying to drag the dance's movements down into the world of things—paper and lines. Measures, time. He sat very still with paper and pencil and summoned up invisible dancers in his mind.

In Banaras, I broke up with the boy I'd followed and left the city more bewildered than I came. I filled my thesis with theory—abstract and beautiful and mostly not my own. Maybe I sensed that I couldn't even articulate the real question I wanted to ask, that only many years later would it come to me.

For years, the ghost fists pummeled through me, then instantly I forgot. Each time, it was the same—like waking from the sort of dream where you remember, for a moment, that you've been dreaming the same dream for weeks, years, that it runs like a current just beneath your days.

But eventually, you do remember. Maybe it was a gradual remembering or maybe it happened all at once, but one day, I could hold the ghost fists still at the corner of my eye. Searching the Internet for *ghost fists* and *feelings of being punched* revealed little, although one site did promise: "Ghosts won't hurt you." And it was true in a way—already the fists were vanishing. As soon as they existed in language, outside me, they no longer really existed at all.

"Time," said John Archibald Wheeler, the physicist who coined the term *black hole*, "is Nature's way of keeping everything from happening at once." By which he meant, perhaps, that the world appears and appears again. We see it as one particular arrangement of things—objects, bodies, molecules—and then another. We call these configurations *moments*. We string one to the next.

My stepsister and I didn't speak much the year we lived in the same house. We'd each fallen into our own separate silence. Sometimes I thought these silences fit together in a way I couldn't yet grasp, a jigsaw of something unknowable. Years later, my stepsister emailed me in India to say she'd written me a letter and it had been sitting on the attic stairs for months, waiting for me. She said, *also the letter I didn't send was in response to a few drawings of yours left in a MOMA catalogue—a matisse woman and a cabinet. do you remember?* I didn't remember. When I was sixteen, I'd left for good. By the time I was in India, that year felt like another life. And yet, my stepsister had unearthed some relic from that time, *responded* to it. Something I'd drawn on paper had traveled through time. I don't know how many hours I spent trying to remember the Matisse woman and the cabinet. She never sent the letter.

Decades after his death, Nijinsky's score for the *Faun* was unearthed from the British Library. To reconstruct the dance as Nijinsky had written it, the notes had first to be decoded. How do you decipher a private language? Nijinsky's notes and sketches were compared to photographs, reviews, firsthand accounts of the time. After a falling-out between Nijinksy and the Ballets Russes' director (they'd been sleeping together), the company stopped performing Nijinsky's dances, and most of them were lost. And yet the *Faun* had survived—passed down not via notation but from dancer to dancer, body to body. Once reconstructed, however, it turned out that the differences between the memory-based ballet and the reconstructed one were great. Hand movements sharpened or slowed, a suddenness was introduced. In memory, of course, we're always changing the movements. We position and reposition the limbs. And who's to say this remembered version isn't truer?

These days, my stepsister doesn't come to the city. It's too loud, she says. Too quick. But sometimes still I put my name in for the lottery at Lincoln Center or find myself sitting across from some small stage in the East Village. I sit in the dark and watch dancers flit in and out of the light. Once I watched a troupe dressed in black move like Chinese characters across the stage, their hands and feet dipped in paint. They tumbled up and down a scroll of parchment like living calligraphy. I was so struck by this, I asked my editor if I could interview the young choreographer. When I went to meet him in his studio, he told me he'd written the entire dance by locking himself in his apartment for several days, lying very still and studying the way breath moved through his body. Then he said, as if from nowhere, "I have been driven by connection."

Maybe there's something troubling about the idea of putting movement to paper—the idea that the body and its trajectory could be fashioned into a kind of hieroglyph, a mark made in space and time. As though we might remember every breath, every turn, every rush of blood to the lungs. As though we might project them into the future. Maybe we don't like to admit how much secret hope we place in this idea—that the body's movement might be its own inscription; that just our being might embody every word, every unsent letter.

Walking around the city, I twist my hair around my finger—one of my stepsister's gestures. And for a second, a trace of her is here. What marks this gesture as hers rather than mine? Nothing except attention—the very act of noticing. Nothing except the feeling: *Please don't go*.

The night before my first article appeared in the newspaper, I couldn't sleep. I was living in Harlem then and found myself pulled out of bed, walking down the street. But it was 4 a.m. and no newsstand was open. I kept walking. I walked so far it was Midtown and then suddenly I knew where I was going. A strange sensation overtook me as I looked up at Port Authority across the street: *I am me*, I thought, *the same me still*. Light was just beginning to hit the buildings all around. I stared up at them, time travelers among us.

In my stepsister's cramped room in the halfway house, I sit amid giant stacks of library books. She picks one up and reads me something she's underlined: *This is the core of all movement. All life fluctuates between the resistance and yielding to gravity.* It's getting dark, and I know I have to leave soon, but I want to ask her something. "Do you remember that year," I start, then don't know how to finish. My stepsister says what she always says: she doesn't remember a lot of things. I try to think of how it must be, not remembering. Lately,

I can't remember my dreams, though I feel them leaving me in the early morning hours. I wake remembering the feeling of struggle, knowing something of great significance has just passed through me.

It's hard to leave her. Standing outside, a part of me wants to grab her hand and whisper: *Come with me—escape*. But of course she can leave the halfway house anytime she wants to; there's nothing holding her here. Instead, I clutch her little painted card—*S.E.A.R.C.H.*—and drive the long way back to the city in the dark, flushed and confused and in love all over again. When I get home, I see she's already emailed me: *you have moved out into the world and i am on a walk toward wellness. we are all fine for now.*

What is a choreography? Maybe it's only the thing that keeps you in time—tells you when to follow, when to turn. Moves you from one moment to the next. The gesture: *Here you are, here.* Someone pulling on your second toe.

I know, wrote Nijinsky, *that the moon is covered in water. I know that astronomers have seen canals. I understand the meaning of canals. I know that people used the canals as a means of escape.*

The last time I crept up to the attic, right before I left my father's house for good, I went around touching my stepsister's things. I searched for a lost message—a sign, a clue. I lay down on her bed and tried to see things as she might have seen them. But I could see only the wall, the window, the close attic light of sky and trees. I watched as the light moved across the room.

But then I did find something. It was buried deep in a stack of papers, softened by time. Of all the many drawings I'd made for my stepsister as a child, this was the one she'd kept: the witch's lair.

Holding it in my hands, I felt again all I'd tried to impart at eight: the feeling the attic had spurred in my chest, the great billowing rooms it opened and closed inside me. I'd forgotten about the river—how it ran behind and through the room. It could drown you, this current, or it could spit you out somewhere on the other side of yourself. By this time, I'd moved on from Plath to Virginia Woolf. When I pictured my own attic, my own raft at sea, I thought of Virginia walking down into the water. But I was different, I thought. I would keep walking. The river wasn't a river but a tunnel—a canal, an escape. Hidden like magmatic water on the moon. If you kept going far enough, you'd reach the other side.

Or maybe, if you were lucky, you'd wash up on the shore, someone pulling on your second toe. Someone tugging you back to this world, the world of things. As if to say: here is the world of bodies, of light. Of all the things light touches. Someone calling you back.

NAUSICAA

Your letter took months to reach me, and when it finally did, it seemed a kind of paper miracle, fragile and improbable. How you scrawled these words on paper, and how they flew folded across oceans and continents, emerged from the black hole of the Indian postal system. How they traveled the labyrinths of Banaras's unnamed alleys and found the one where David and I lived, in a crumbling apartment that let in the dust and the ants. How when I opened the letter, your words spilled out: *OK, so I'm old-fashioned and mostly one-handed.*

You died once, you liked to say. You may have died twice. At this, your mustache twitched with a secret grin—you had a secret grin for many things you liked to say. When your letter came to me, I was twenty years old, living in Banaras, India. Halfway around the world, in Philadelphia, you were sixty, driving a secondhand limo. This was the same limo that would appear some mornings outside my childhood house, those mornings you used to drive me to high school. What did we talk about during those drives? I can't remember now. In those days, I was also a person who believed I had died. I spent my days floating, dislodged from my skin. Did you tell me I would live, despite having already died? Or maybe this was just what I gleaned from you: you chain-smoking in the driver's seat, you cracking jokes and steering with your knees. The brain tumor that nearly killed you had left you with a limp—the one sign of your once or maybe twice dying. Did you tell me that a dead person, especially, has to write things down? *OK, so I'm old-fashioned and mostly one-handed, but I think of you often.* Your signature was a mustached and bowler-capped face.

I didn't write you back right away. Instead, I walked the city and talked to myself. Or I talked to some version of myself, and sometimes that person was you. I liked to think these dispatches would reach you faster and clearer anyway.

In the alleys where the silk weavers worked, the city quieted to a whisper. Tangles of colored thread pooled in the gutters or hung from the mess of electric wires like strange, tropical birds. All around me, I'd hear the clicking of looms.

At night, the bats flew in, blind as the dark. David and I could hear them getting caught in the ceiling fan. The blades flung their bodies like tiny, bloodied sacks against the walls and sometimes into our bed. Or the electricity would go out and then we'd hear the whole city breathing at once. The alley snored its familiar snores: the woman who sighed in the same key each night, the old man who coughed the same cough and spit. In the dark, you could hear how close we were.

You liked winding roads the best. You avoided interstates and highways. You drove me to high school because sometimes I didn't have another way and you were afraid I might just stop going. Some days we talked and some days we didn't. Really, we knew each other through reading. You gave me books to read and read the things I wrote. *You know how to turn a sentence.* When I was eighteen, you gave me *Ulysses.*

In *Ulysses*, too, people are always winding through streets—missing one another or colliding, scarcely knowing the odd ways they overlap.

For years, you were a reader at the Philadelphia Bloomsday. Your chapter was Nausicaa. You'd look up from the book every now and then to crack lewd jokes, and once, the one time I saw you read, you looked out to the very last row, where your wife and I sat, and winked. I can see it, even now. Something about this look stops me: some bent in your eyes, a laugh that clamors all the way across time. And then how your face turned as you made your way offstage, fingers still wedged between pages, your bad leg dragging softly behind you.

When I was young, I used to have reading dreams—strange in-between dreams, the text streaming in lines before me. I'd follow the words blindly, not quite knowing what I was doing or why. And then finally I'd see that I was reading. But the moment the words became words to me, they disappeared.

In Banaras, I'd fallen into a kind of exile. Like Leopold Bloom, I wandered the streets. I drifted along the river and through the alleys, avoiding my apartment—the dust, the ants, the fights with David. They were the sort of black-hole fights we emerged from blinking and numb, not quite knowing who we were or where, and it took acts ever more spectacular to send us stumbling out. He threw a book at my head. I locked myself in the bathroom all night. So like the thousands of pilgrims who came to Banaras each day, I made my way through alleys cracked with time. Banaras was a maze, I sometimes thought. Or maybe time itself was the maze, always coming undone.

The pilgrims prayed as they walk. They came to seek *darshan*—seeing. An exchange between the eyes of the beholder and the divine. I saw eyes of the divine everywhere: in statues and effigies, drawn on paper and stuck to tree shrines. When a statue was finished, the deity's breath was called down into it and a needle pierced open its eyes.

I didn't know how to pray, but I too was hungry for seeing. I was trying to see my way into things. Or I was trying to look and look until I didn't know what it was I saw.

At the other end of our alley lived a girl with crooked teeth. From our roof, I sometimes saw her standing in her doorway, naming the dogs that passed in the night.

In Banaras, David and I were doing our coursework remotely, typing up term papers in dingy Internet cafés and sending them off to our small liberal arts school in New England. We were both scholarship students at the sort of freethinking, bohemian school where this was possible—the kind of place where everyone lived out in the woods or in strange huts that looked like spaceships. Where people wore artfully ragged clothing and where I felt awash in beautiful ideas but also amiss: vulgar and somehow wrong in the painterly New England quiet. I knew I didn't really belong. I liked David because he gave every appearance of belonging—loud and gregarious and moving effortlessly between groups—but secretly, I knew, he was like me: marked by places and events unspeakable in this pristine little world. And maybe that was why he'd followed me to this city on the other side of the world. In Banaras, people were always asking him about his studies, commending me for tagging along with him. But in fact, I was the one who was always going; I'd decided to write my thesis on divine iconography, and it was only at the last minute that David said he was coming, that he didn't want to be without me.

On a whim, I'd signed up for a class on Joyce, and I decided to write my final paper on Nausicaa. I'd never asked why that was your favorite chapter. It seemed obvious to me at the time: *Ulysses* at its most tender and most obscene—Leopold Bloom masturbating to the young Gerty MacDowell on the beach. *Darling, I saw your. I saw all.* And yet, Bloom has a way of not just seeing but seeing *into*. He winds his way into the glancings of others: passersby, objects, cats. Nausicaa begins in Gerty's head and ends in Bloom's. Or is he imagining her thoughts as he watches? I never knew—I was always caught in the space between.

The first time you were dying, you downed gin in your hospital bed, making passes at all the nurses. Even dying, you were a flirt. I didn't know you then. One day, years later, you saw me reading a book of T.S. Eliot poems. I was fourteen, and you were a friend of my parents'—the man with the limo and giant mustache. Which is to say you weren't real to me yet. I suspect I wasn't real to you. But that day you sat at the kitchen table and wanted to know which was my favorite poem. *Prufrock*, I said. You leaned back and started reciting: *Let us go then, you and I, when the evening is spread out against the sky like a patient*—you sat waiting, expectantly, but I couldn't summon up the rest. *Like a patient etherized upon a table!* you exclaimed finally, gesturing widely and telling me to learn the words by heart. But I don't know that I understood what it was to know things by heart—for words to cut and cut so close they entered *into* the body. I didn't understand, for that matter, what it was to be a body, etherized upon a table.

The most sacred places to receive darshan were known as *tirthas*—crossings. Banaras was one such crossing—an opening, it was said, into another world. I'd walk the ghats, the stone steps that stretched along the Ganges and disappeared down into the water. The pilgrims prayed on the ghats. They bathed in the river and slapped laundry against rocks. They watched the burning of the dead. Banaras was a place where people came to die, the dead crossing into the next world by way of the river, Shiva whispering into their ears. To die there was to slip past the cycles of death and rebirth, to wash straight through to *moksha*.

I first read *Ulysses* in a weeklong fever of reading. You gave me the book—one of your own copies—and a cassette tape, which I wasn't supposed to listen to until the very end. I was eighteen and took the bus back to college in a snowstorm. In my dorm room, I sat pressed up against the window, reading, while the world erased itself outside. I read so hard my eyes hurt. I read so hard I thought I might've been going blind, as Joyce did. I read all day and most nights, barely sleeping, and when I came finally to Molly Bloom's soliloquy—to that last *yes I said yes I will Yes*—the sun was just coming up over the snow.

Later, in Banaras, I'd hear the story of Krishna, how his mother opened his mouth and saw the universe lodged in his throat. She saw the world, full of lightning and wind and rain. She saw her own village, and inside it, she saw herself. This is how it is sometimes to finish a very long book. The world was outside my window. The world pricked inside my throat. The world was everywhere, everywhere at once. Then I remembered the cassette tape. I pressed play, and a woman's voice trembled from my speakers, half-drowned and otherworldly: Molly's soliloquy. She drew out the first word like a magician's scarf pulled tremulously from air: *Yes*.

The pilgrims came in cycles, according to rhythms of various and overlapping cosmologies. One day, a procession of women streamed through our alley on the way to Lolark Kund—dark steps leading straight down to an ancient gleam of water. From morning until dark, the women filled the alley. They came for two days, and on the third day, they were gone. In the movement of the pilgrims, a hidden city sometimes became visible. In Banaras, new constellations of holy sites emerge or re-emerge after centuries, new rhymes of worship co-alesce or fall away. The pilgrims write these patterns with their feet. They write and rewrite.

For the pilgrims, darshan is also a kind of contact—a movement of the seeing toward the seen. Sight goes forth and touches the deity, briefly assuming its form.

When the pupils focus on an object, David told me once, it becomes the sole point of attention. This is why we look into space when thinking, he said. To look at something is to be subsumed by it. To see is to become the thing one sees.

Between the ghats, the alleys looped and mazed, and in them, I believed wild and impossible things. One day, I saw Hebrew letters on a sign and believed for a moment I'd come across a lost tribe of Israel—of course they would be here, I thought, in this ruined city on the Ganges. Then I saw that the sign was pointing the way to an Israeli hostel. Or I retraced my footsteps and found myself eye to eye with a giant, blinking cow where there'd been no cow a moment before. In the alleys, the cows never moved, only appeared. Gangs of monkeys lurched from roof to roof. Boys jumped over sleeping beggars. The girl with the crooked teeth smiled shyly from her doorway. Rounding a corner, I saw an old man reach into the sunken cavern of his chest and pull out his own heart.

One morning, Vimal-ji, the clay-wallah, taught me how to make little clay birds: how to turn teardrop-shaped bits of clay into things with beaks and wings. I was always hanging around his shop, watching him make things. His statues emerged in time with the festival seasons: a hundred Durgas for Durga Puja, two hundred Lakshmis during Divali. Vimal-ji sat cross-legged beside a giant pit in the floor and summoned these figures out of inchoate gray slabs, torsos and limbs squirming into view. When he finished, he said a prayer and pierced open their eyes.

I was walking back through the alleys with my clumsy little birds when the girl with the crooked teeth leaned across her stoop and stopped me. She motioned to the birds in my hands, pointing until I understood that I was to give them to her. *Khal malinge*, she said. *See you tomorrow.* The next day, she was waiting, arms behind her back. She leaned again across the stoop to show me. Clutched in her hands were my birds, painted now and bright. She motioned me toward her stone doorway, and I wondered briefly why she wasn't in school. But already I was moving out of the trembling dust and heat, stepping into a darkness so worn I seemed to know it somehow already, and for a second I was sure it had been waiting for me—this doorway, this room, this girl with a handful of birds—as though I'd finally come to grasp the strange and pulsing thing inside my chest.

She was Mouli, short for Moulshri, but at first we heard it as Molly. She was fourteen, tall and dreamy-eyed. She was always standing in the doorway, motioning David and me inside. In the evenings, David would sit on the stoop with Mouli's father, Rajesh, playing long games of chess. The electricity was always cutting out and then they played by candlelight, Rajesh passing a whiskey bottle through the dark. Mouli's mother stayed late at the temple, praying. Her older brother slept. Mouli gave me her English homework to look over or brought down trinkets and pictures from the shelf above her bed. *Gods*, she pointed.

Dolls. Some gods were tiny plastic statues. Others were bright, cartoon-ish pictures clipped from calendars and magazines. The dolls were actual dolls or they were sacks of rice with hand-drawn mouths and eyes. One was a balloon. Each had a name, a birthday. Mouli pointed to one after the next: *Krishna, Choti, Hanuman, Grandma, Baby Brother Who Died, Shiva, Dog Sheru, Dog Kiki.* One English assignment asked about her future. In the space next to *career,* she'd written *astronaut.*

After David and I stumbled back through the dark alley to our apartment, I'd climb up to the roof. I thought of people on the other side of the world making their way through daylight. I pictured them as though from far away—from space maybe—and they looked tiny as ants, crawling through a dream city. You were there, of course, winding through the streets in your limo or puttering around your apartment. You tended to your many plants or cooked your wife elaborate meals. You fed the cat. You reached for a book on the shelf. I wondered which.

I decided that my term paper would be about looking. Nausicaa, after all, is a chapter told in glances and gazes, odd snatches of seeing. Bloom looks at Gerty and Gerty looks back. They look and then look away. *She let him and she saw that he saw.* They see each other in the smallest of moments—half-glimpses always disappearing.

Sometimes the bats flew in while David and I were asleep, and then we'd find their bodies the next morning, bloodied and covered with ants. The summer before we left for India, we'd been taking Hindi classes and living in an airless attic apartment. One night, two bats flung themselves across the living room and we crashed around the apartment trying to chase them out. *A sign,* we'd joke later.

There were days that summer when David couldn't walk. It would happen very suddenly. Or his hands and feet would turn numb. One night, we drove to the emergency room, which set in motion a battery of doctors and specialists, scans and MRIs. There was a call—there's always a call. I was standing in line for my oral Hindi exam when I saw David's name on my phone. His voice was a traveling abyss. *They said it's all over my brain.* Minutes passed. Words must have passed between us too, but when I walked into the Hindi exam room a few minutes later, I found I couldn't speak. My tongue had laid down in my mouth like something dead.

The next day, a neurologist pointed to ghostly white blurs all along David's brain and spine. He showed us a map of nerves. *Primary progressive multiple sclerosis*, he said. The white spots looked like blurs in old photographs—faces moving too fast for light.

Death-think, I started calling the way my mind worked in the days after. Everything impossible and exquisite in its ordinariness—a glass jar, a scratched cabinet—all of it suffused with a crumbling sort of light. The diagnosis wasn't a death sentence, of course, but it felt that way at the time. There was no way of saying how the ghost spots would eddy at David's nervous system, how fast or how slow. Still, I looked out the window as we drove home from the neurologist's and wondered how I'd failed to register so many things in the world, which now seemed wholly contingent on my noticing. David, meanwhile, got into bed and didn't come out for two weeks.

The most famous moment of seeing happens late in *Ulysses*, deep into night. It's a moment of seeing between Bloom and Stephen Dedalus—the book's unknowing Odysseus and Telemachus. Bloom's own son died as an infant years earlier. Stephen has recently lost his mother. They are both in kinds of exile. If Stephen is the young artist, Bloom is the middle-aged everyman. He delights in the physical world—he is *of* the world—while Stephen, abstract and cerebral, looks in from outside it. They spend the course of the day winding through the city, crossing paths, mostly missing each other. But at the end of the night, it's Bloom who picks Stephen up after a drunken brawl and brings him home. They talk in Bloom's kitchen, and as they go out into the night, about to part ways, there's a brief moment in which they both see the same thing.

What spectacle confronted them when they, first the host, then the guest emerged silently, doubly dark, from obscurity by a passage from the rere of the house into the penumbra of the garden?

The heaventree of stars hung with humid nightblue fruit.

The day I finished *Ulysses* was also the day I met David. For the longest time, I thought of the two things as linked—as though he'd somehow emerged from those pages, or the book had slipped me through to a world where he existed. The night we met, it was another snowstorm, and the fire alarm had broken in my dorm, sirening for hours and casting me out into the snow. David, who lived off campus, had been stranded, and we found ourselves marooned in a dark building screening a black-and-white French film. We sat against the back wall, the subtitles too far away to read. David was twenty-seven, a former ballet dancer who'd just now returned to school. He'd danced with companies in New York and London and, for a while, in San Francisco, the city where I'd found myself at fifteen, a runaway. Was he there when I was there? Yes, we determined. If we'd passed each other on the street, would we have recognized something in each other? It seemed possible. Did we embellish the stories of our travels—his dancing, my running away—to get at some bigger truth? Likely. Places became stories, and the gaps between these stories became more stories, until finally talking began to resemble a map, everywhere leading everywhere at once. Did we stare straight ahead as though on a very long road trip, talking about things we'd remember or forget, and did we believe, secretly, we'd go on talking this way forever?

At night in Banaras, lying awake, I could hear the needle like a trigger clicking. A nurse had taught both of us how. *In case David can't one day*, she insisted, though I had a terrible fear of needles. This was how the world was, I'd think, lying awake: always the thing you fear most winding up in the same bed as you. Most nights, I looked away.

The dust got inside us. It got inside our fingernails, nostrils. It turned everything black. In one *purana*, the city itself is a body. The smaller river Asi is its head and various ghats are its chest, thighs, and feet. We lived at Tulsi Ghat, just below Asi. The city was a body, I'd sometimes think, and we were lodged in its throat.

Mouli and I sat on the stoop one night talking. *Why do you want to be an astronaut?* I asked. She thought for a minute and said in Hindi: *There was a woman in a spaceship*. I nodded, not understanding. *There was a woman in a spaceship and it exploded above the Earth*. She meant Kalpana Chawla on the space shuttle *Columbia*, I realized. *Explosion*, Mouli said again, using the English word and pointing at the sky. We both looked up.

There was a legend about a network of tunnels running beneath the city. Centuries ago, it was said, the Brahmans had used them to get to the river unpolluted by the streets. It was true that the streets were sometimes very bad: hands reached out from crowds to grab me; I once got pushed into an open sewer. But this wasn't why I liked to think about the tunnels. Mostly, I liked to believe in a city beneath the city, an aliveness running just below us, unseen. I wanted to believe there was more, more than I could see.

In the days you drove me to high school, I didn't think I'd live very long. If I was alive at all, it seemed an unlikely reprieve. I couldn't imagine living to thirty. It was impossible to sleep at my house, impossible to get away from the noise of shouting, glass breaking. I stayed up most of the night pacing around my room, sometimes scribbling things down—poems, plays—but more often feeling unmoored from my skin, an astronaut looking down at a tiny body from space. After one sleepless night, I stumbled into your passenger seat barely awake and then caught a glimpse of myself in the sideview mirror. My face was pocked with small white spots: toothpaste, which was supposed to be good for pimples. I'd forgotten to wash them off. I blushed a blush that stayed with me for weeks.

For the middle-aged Bloom, time has become worn and circular—everything harkens back. *So it returns*, he thinks. *Think you're escaping and run into yourself. Longest way round is the shortest way home.* Gerty, meanwhile, is young enough to feel the world hasn't happened to her yet. She thinks of herself as *something aloof, apart in another sphere.* She describes herself in the lacquered vernacular of Victorian novels and women's magazines. She writes poetry. She takes note of Bloom watching her and weaves him into her narrative—a foreigner, a stranger, her one true love.

But there's also a glimpse of Gerty earlier in the day, hours before she appears on the beach. She's on an errand for her father, who is laid up, it's said, a drunk. Later, in Nausicaa: *She had even witnessed in the home circle deeds of violence.* All the mornings you drove me to school, we never talked about my family. Your letter came close. *I know you grew up in far from ideal situations.* The plural tugged at me: *situations.* We never talked about it, but somehow I was sure you knew everything—even the things you couldn't possibly have known. Now I wonder not how much you knew but why it mattered so much to me, at seventeen, to believe you knew everything about me.

Sometimes I think I might have invented you. We're always inventing each other, in a way. We need witnesses. We need witnesses—not many, even just one—to the impossibly long sentence we write with our days.

Mouli's house was divided into two rooms. Her older brother was away working for weeks at a time or he lay sleeping on the bed that doubled as a couch. We never knew what it was he did, exactly, but when he returned, Rajesh stayed out all night drinking. They never seemed to have any money.

Don't you have school? we asked Mouli when we passed her in the daytime. *Late*, she said, flattening laundry on the stoop. When he was awake, Rajesh chimed in: *Time is for the British. No time in Banaras.*

I first thought I'd go to India when I was seventeen—not to Banaras but to the Narmada River. I'd read about a dam forcing people from their villages, and how they'd vowed to stay and drown. I became obsessed with this story. I dreamed about it. I would go there too, I thought. It seemed the only possible way of being in the world: to hurl myself against it until water rose above my head.

One day, I met a sadhu on the ghats. The sadhus were holy men, perpetual pilgrims who walked the city dressed in orange robes. Mostly they walked right by me, staring out into the distance with a kind of pained concentration. But this one smiled. His skin was parched and worn. A long white beard hung almost to his ribs. When he spoke, it was in a peculiarly accented English. *Hello, young lady.* This was Govinda Baba, I realized. Among Banaras's tiny expat population, he was something of a legend. He'd come to India as a backpacker in 1968 and never left. Now he told me how he'd thrown his passport into the Ganges. *I came to Banaras looking for God*, he said, in the way of someone who'd told this story many times. *I thought God was something I could put in my backpack and go home.* He laughed and gazed out at the river. *So what happened?* I asked, expecting more. He shrugged. *I was wrong.*

In the weeks that David lay in bed, I sat in the window smoking his cigarettes, unable to sleep. I was afraid for David, yes, but I was also afraid for myself. David wasn't someone who could just get into bed and not come out—not the David I knew. In the end, of course, he did come out, and then he was the same David he'd always been. Or this was how it seemed to me. Maybe it was the gap that always exists between two people, or maybe it was the way that gap is widened, infinitely, by illness. If for me death-think was something that could come and go, for David this was what it was now to be a body. And a body is always a locked thing—no exit from it. Yes, of course we would still go to India, we told people. Of course we would go to India and to Banaras, in particular. If there was something strange about this city we were bound for—a place where people came to die—we didn't dwell on it at the time.

On Divali, Mouli tied red string bracelets around our wrists. *For long life*, she said, and I burst, inexplicably, into tears. I didn't know if I was crying for David or for me or for the very idea of living a long life, which I now believed I might.

There's a theory about the *Odyssey*'s Princess Nausicaa, the one who saves Odysseus when he's lost at sea. The writer Samuel Butler claimed that she was the epic's secret author—that it wasn't Homer who wrote the *Odyssey*, but a girl on the coast of Sicily, writing herself into the poem as the princess. Most of Butler's contemporaries laughed him off, but he gained a cult following, and his books found their way to Joyce's shelves.

Of course, Joyce's own Nausicaa, Gerty, doesn't feed and clothe her Odysseus. She doesn't take him to meet her father, the king. Instead, she watches the sun go down and reads *Princess novelette*, a magazine. She daydreams impossible things. She lets Bloom watch her. She watches back.

The fights between me and David grew worse. He pushed me into a wall, and I moved briefly into a guesthouse on Asi Ghat. Our fights no longer seemed real to me. They'd taken on the quality of dreams: bodies in motion, unable to stop. He always found me, and I always came back.

Once I brought David to your apartment. I'd wanted you to meet him. But you caught him off guard with a question, something about his family, and his chin jutted forward. *I never even think about it*, he lied. *It's such a long time ago.* At this, you looked at me and winked, jerked your fist up and down—masturbation, you meant.

One night, David and I went over to a friend's house to watch a movie. He was a Czech doctoral student who'd brought from home an extensive collection of non-Bollywood DVDs—a rare commodity in Banaras. It took a minute to realize why the movie looked familiar. It was the French film, the one from the night in the snowstorm. We sat watching, able now to read the subtitles, and I wondered if Banaras was the place where everything eventually caught up with you, where the stubborn rhymes of your life eternally recurred. *No time in Banaras.* In the movie, someone said: *It was an affair that could only exist in the violence of trench warfare, with death always nearby.* At the end, the woman drove herself off a bridge.

There's a touch of the artist about old Bloom, says a man on the street, recalling how Bloom once pointed out all the constellations in the night sky. But really, there's a touch of the artist about almost everyone in *Ulysses*—not just Stephen, the young artist, but Molly, who sings, and Gerty with her poetry. They're people who can't help but make things. Little pieces of the world come loose and they hold them up to the light.

David didn't love books the way I did, but he liked the idea of writing. His father was from Mississippi, a black man who'd grown up an orphan, raised by strangers, and who, at sixteen, lied about his age and did two tours of duty in Vietnam. Late in life, he'd started writing about the war—two memoirs and a novel. He simply sat down one day, David said, and wrote with great haste, as though he wanted to get down all the things he'd never said in life. And sometimes, late at night, David wrote me long, dream-like emails out of nowhere: *I thought I was writing to myself, but now I think I'm writing to you. You are the person I'm always talking to even when I'm talking to myself.*

At night, the city dreamed—strange in-between dreams. Packs of dogs moved through the alleys. The pilgrims turned in their sleep. The chai-wallah closed his stall like a box all around him, TV light seeping through the cracks. On nights when the electricity went out, before our eyes adjusted there was a moment when the city shut itself like a box full of dark. In this moment, we saw nothing. All of us at once.

A darkness flits through the space between Bloom and Gerty. *Hither, thither, with a tiny lost cry.* A bat.

In April, your tumor came back. It pressed on your eye so you couldn't see anymore. I sat down finally to write you a letter and then realized you wouldn't be able to read it.

There was a round of chemotherapy. The odds weren't good, your wife said in an email. But you had died before and come back; you always came back. When, afterward, they gave you four weeks to live, I still didn't believe it. I walked the alleys believing wild and impossible things. My red string bracelet had stayed around my wrist, improbably, all year—long after David's and Mouli's had fallen off. I decided this meant you'd stay alive.

I opened *Ulysses*. Maybe I thought I could read my way back to you. Or maybe you'd left some clue, something I hadn't noticed the first time—an underlining, a note. But it was only my own unsteady underlinings, my dumb scribblings in the margins. Then I turned a page and something fluttered to the ground: a thin white prescription from a doctor's pad, its script illegible. I remembered finding it when I was eighteen and placing it back between the pages, choosing to believe it was yours, though, really, who knew who read that book before you, before me?

Much like Bloom does with Stephen, you once offered me a place to stay—one night, like many nights, when I didn't want to go home. I lay on your couch, unsleeping but suffused with a strange, wide calm, as though the night were a lake and also the thing that could ferry me across. You woke up early—you always woke up early—so early it was dark still. You passed by the couch, and for a second we looked at each other. You saw that I was awake, and I saw that you saw. Then I lay there listening as you moved through the kitchen, the noise of you keeping me company in the dark.

You could speak less and less, your wife said, your sentences ungathering. You sat on the balcony with your plants, your cat. I pictured you reading, then remembered you couldn't. But if you knew the words by heart, I thought, you could move through them even blind. They could keep you company in the dark.

Some said the words Shiva whispered into the ears of the dying were the *taraka*, or ferryboat mantra. Death, they said, was a time of great danger and intense light—whatever separated this shore from the final shore at once far and thin. But it was just words, finally, the boat that carried one across.

You died in bed with your wife. You were napping together, and when she woke, you had gone. I read this in an email at the Internet café on Asi Ghat. You died in the morning, but in Banaras it was night. Suddenly I wished I had a picture of you. And because I didn't know what else to do, I typed the words *Leopold Bloom* into the search engine, believing, for a second, they would get me to you.

I found my red bracelet on the floor the next morning. It had broken off in the night.

I kept talking to you.

In dreams, things may go missing, but in the morning they're still there. I lost the cassette tape you gave me, the one with Molly Bloom's soliloquy. *But somewhere it must still exist,* I thought, her voice still speaking into some corner of the universe. I wondered how long your voice would stay alive inside me.

In other dreams, it's the missing things that come back. I kept thinking I'd see you one night in a dream.

But when I dreamt of you finally, it was like my childhood dreams of reading. The moment I understood who you were, you disappeared. *I will have to become my own witness now*, I thought.

Except in reading, you didn't travel far or wide. You stayed close to Philadelphia your whole life. Toward the end, you made a pilgrimage of sorts to Jerusalem, which surprised me. You were not particularly religious, though you had a grandfather, Leopold, who'd been a Hebraic scholar, and his volumes of the Talmud lined your shelves. The Talmud, of course, is also a text of exile, and it too endeavors to swallow the whole world. Bloom, meanwhile, is estranged not just from Molly but, as a Jew, from Ireland, and Joyce himself wrote most of *Ulysses* not in Dublin but in Trieste and Zurich. The Talmud also marks the point at which the Jews became the proverbial people of the book. Cast out from Jerusalem after the destruction of the Temple, the center of oral scholarship, they began to wander. And what can wandering people hold onto but words?

Just before he takes Stephen home, Bloom has a vision of his dead son, Rudy, as he might look at eleven. He's holding a book and reading, it's suggested, in Hebrew. *He reads from right to left inaudibly, smiling, kissing the page.* When Bloom calls his name, he gazes, unseeing, into his father's eyes, then goes on reading, kissing, smiling.

One day, a month before we left Banaras, Rajesh asked David and me for money to fix Mouli's teeth. Or rather, he asked David. *So she can find a good husband*, he said. Already he might not be able to afford a dowry. David and I debated the implications of this for many hours and finally agreed to give the money. But when David asked how much it would cost, Rajesh wouldn't give him an answer. *Give as you wish*, he said. This went back and forth for weeks. We wanted to give the right amount, we said. In truth, I didn't really believe the money would go to Mouli's teeth, but I wanted to give it anyway, just in case. David insisted that we at least get a number. *As you wish, as you wish*, said Rajesh. The day we were supposed to leave drew nearer, but still there was no answer.

We had one last fight the night before we left. The next day, David would leave for a summer job in China and I would go back to New England. Maybe we knew we wouldn't see each other again. All the furniture had been sold, all our things were packed. The apartment was empty except for the two of us: two bodies caught between its walls. David flung the entire contents of my suitcase across the room.

I lay, unsleeping, on the floor. I tried to picture you existing in some other form—a handful of glowing atoms, smoke from a pyre. I was always trying and failing. I put everything back into my suitcase and went down to Tulsi Ghat because it was too hot to sleep. It was four in the morning, but already the first temple bells were ringing and women were bathing in the dark water. A sadhu sat praying in the distance. Above, there were blossoms, stars—some strange friction of permanent and impermanent things.

If I saw you at all, I saw you wandering through sentences, words rising up like crooked overhangs on narrow streets. *The heaventree of stars hung with humid nightblue fruit.*

For a minute, it seemed possible: that if a sentence stayed with you all your life, it could pierce through to you, even dead. Even if it appeared only like dream words—perfectly known and unreadable.

Or say your life was the sentence—one you turned and turned until one day even you, your own most secret author, could read what it was it said.

Your letter told me to keep writing. *But for who now?* I wondered.

In Trieste, the twenty-five-year-old Joyce befriended Ettore Schmitz, a middle-aged Italian man of Jewish origin. Several years later, when Joyce's writing had stalled, Schmitz wrote him a letter urging him to finish *A Portrait of the Artist as a Young Man*. But perhaps more importantly, Schmitz also envisioned *a whole novel of everyday life*. Joyce was already in the planning stages of *Ulysses*—what would become his book of a single day and everything inside it. Of course, it's impossible to know the degree to which Joyce was influenced by Schmitz, who later became known by his penname, Italo Svevo. But it was a picture of Schmitz—not his own father—that hung for years above Joyce's desk.

All our belongings were piled into a rickshaw when we stopped for the last time in front of Mouli's house. The midmorning light cut into us, everywhere we looked a kind of wince. Rajesh took David aside, and I knew of course what he was asking. I watched as David slowly shook his head. Later, in the rickshaw, he'd tell me that Rajesh had asked: *Are you forgetting something?* Mouli and I, meanwhile, reprised a longstanding joke. I'd asked her once what movie she wanted to see, and she rattled off the latest Shahrukh Khan film, *Kabhi Alvida Naa Kehna*, which then became our standard parting. Literally, *We Must Never Say Goodbye*. Then she looked at me, suddenly serious. *No, no. You, me. Kabhi alvida naa kehna.*

Are you forgetting something? I asked myself all the way to the train station, not knowing, of course, that I'd keep asking forever.

David and I wouldn't see each other again, though one day, many years later, he'd call me up, and we'd talk and talk as if no time had passed. We'd talk this way many nights—about the past, about the future, about the cities we'd someday walk through—until one night he told me I was the love of his life. But he'd be married then, with a family.

I tried to talk him out of it. It was because I was the last one, I said, the last before he was married. It was because I was with him when he got sick. He laughed. I wasn't the last one, he said. And it had nothing to do with getting sick.

For the first time in years, I thought about Nausicaa, Butler's secret author—not a seafarer who traveled far and wide, but a girl stuck on the shore. And how in the poem, she dreams up Odysseus before she meets him: an absence, a possibility, a hole in the universe through which she might slip. I tried to say all this: how we dream up people too. How we gather tiny pieces—gestures, looks—and construct grand, epic figures, people who carry inside them entire worlds. How we look in their throats and see the universe. But David only said: *Why is it so hard for you to believe this?* And of course, a part of me did want to believe, to know exactly what he meant when he said that the first moment he stepped into my college dorm room, he felt time become suddenly very dense. How he looked around, dizzied by the walls—I'd covered every inch with paintings—and how he knew then that an hour, a moment, a day could hold everything inside it.

And for a moment I would know. But only for a moment.

All that, though, would come later. During my last days in Banaras, I was still trying to write my paper on Gerty MacDowell. I was having trouble because I could find few scholarly sources. Gerty had been read mostly as a minor character—overly narrow, subjectified, hemmed in by competing discourses of femininity. But I wanted to write something different. For all her romantic posturing, for all her escapist fantasies, I was more and more convinced that she knew exactly what she was doing. She doesn't just let herself be watched; she looks back. She writes her own story into the looking. As fireworks explode with orgasmic cadence overhead, she raises her skirt up and up her leg.

There's a nakedness about seeing, a blush that never quite goes away. Even when the only other witness is dead.

It's just as Gerty gets up to walk away that the perspective shifts from her to Bloom. Her words begin to falter, and in this faltering we see.

She walked with a certain quiet dignity characteristic of her but with care and very slowly because—because Gerty MacDowell was…

Tight boots? No. She's lame! O!

Mr. Bloom watched her as she limped away.

Sitting by the river that last morning, I thought maybe I'd been misreading our roles all this time. We're never any one thing, after all— always, we're the watcher and the watched. Because suddenly in that moment, I was the one left sitting on the shore. I watched you as you limped away.

It was an image that came to me the night I typed *Leopold Bloom* into a computer on Asi Ghat. (Why is it we want to hold onto a picture when someone dies?) The image was a sketch Joyce made years after he'd finished *Ulysses*, just after an operation had briefly returned his failing eyesight. He picked up a piece of charcoal and drew a man with a bowler hat and a mustache. Beneath it twitched Leopold Bloom's secret grin. Joyce set the charcoal down, picked it up again. He scrawled in Greek the first words of the *Odyssey*.

Tell me, muse, of that man of many turns, who wandered far and wide.

DEAD GIRLS

Tell me what you know about dismemberment.
—Bhanu Kapil

1.

Her name is Gracie. It was Frank's idea to name her—Frank, your dissection partner, a ponytailed Rolfer with a limp. "She looks like a Gracie," he pronounced, pulling back the white sheet.

Two hours later, he asks: "You ever seen somebody like Gracie up close before?" He means somebody dead.

"No," you tell him. "Never." And then you're flooded with a rolling, queasy sensation—the one that feels like lying even when every word is true. Or maybe it's just the reek of formaldehyde, a sick-sweet roiling in your skull. You hear the instructor as though from far away: skin is an organ, he keeps saying, how it pulls and breathes. But all you see is the stunned yellow of Gracie's back, the blunt dead heap of her. Tiny webbed capillaries worm up from the deep.

Four tables, four corpses in the room, formaldehyde-pumped and wobbly. Bald as aliens. They're naked, obviously, but still it shocks you, this nakedness—cold and raw and facedown too. You tell your-self the dead can't be wounded; they're already dead. You make it a joke: *Four corpses walk into a bar.*

You and Frank spent the first half hour stalling, cleaning and reclean-ing utensils. The first instruction seemed easy enough—*Place the ca-daver prone*—but then you mulled over the word *prone*. Was it just a matter of lying down, or were there, in fact, degrees of proneness? Frank said it had to do with the legs, open or closed, and you kept thinking of the thing monks do, or nuns before the cross. Minutes later, you realized that was *prostrate*. Finally, you typed the word into your phone and read out the definition. *One: likely or liable to suffer something, typically something regrettable or unwelcome. Two: lying flat, especially face downward.*

You and Frank stared at the body and then looked up, as though seeing each other for the first time—you who were suddenly supple with life, you who were about to commit regrettable and perhaps unwelcome deeds.

You've enrolled in a four-day anatomy workshop, shelled out a de-posit you couldn't afford, because you've been having panic attacks late into the night. Because you're terrorized by the beating of your own heart, the blood going in and out of your chest, and what would happen if it suddenly stopped? Because yoga made you laugh and acupuncture made you weep, and because you were beginning to think there was something wrong with you.

But the joke's on you, because now you're standing in a room full of yogis and massage therapists. Rolfers like Frank. The sort of people who have long and earnest discussions about deep tissue and somatic memory, hidden geographies beneath the skin. Exactly the people you'd hoped to avoid.

The instructor is a tall, loose-limbed man named Jeremiah who stalks the room and calls you all somanauts—voyagers casting out into inner deep space. But there's nothing astral about it, so far as you can see. You think of it more like spelunking, like cool, dark caves. Once you get past the smell, it's practically intoxicating, like peering inside your own skin.

Jeremiah crosses the country hosting workshops like this one. You picture him like a one-man traveling circus, cadavers in tow. He preaches the subtle beauty of organs, shimmies his arms to illustrate the movements of the heart. In every cut, he says, you're opening a door—a portal into the great beyond. You watch him move through the room, nodding emphatically and making overlong eye contact, and you hope he doesn't turn out to be some sort of cult leader.

Cults have been on your mind lately because of the guru. Two months ago Vik, your boss, gave you a box of cassette tapes to transcribe, old recordings of the guru from the seventies. The guru's young disciples called themselves the Beloved, and Vik had once been one of them, traveling in a bright and wild caravan across India. The tapes are one of his pet projects: an archive of the guru's extemporaneous musings. A project that's been foisted onto you.

A part of you fears that really Vik gave you tapes because he detected in you some sort of spiritual paucity, that he wants to redeem you. Recently he looked up from his computer screen to declare that all people struggle with one of three things: anger, ambition, or lust. "I don't struggle with any of those," you said. In part because it was true and in part because you didn't want to hear where this was going. A week later, you found the tapes on your desk. Vik said he'd pay you extra since transcribing the words of a dead man isn't exactly in your job description.

Your job is to edit a monthly newsletter that calls itself a magazine and occasionally to write, though in truth you've been doing less and less of this lately. Your office is in the UN building, hidden in a decayed and yellowing back hallway. Every morning, you pass through grand foyers blazing with light, long carpeted halls lined with galactic assembly rooms. Then you turn onto the shoddy ruins of the press wing: crowded desks heaped together, halls littered with the guts of discarded computers. You turn once more into the lightless back passageway where they stow the people who barely count as press, like you.

When you told Vik you needed to cut out early a few days this week and the next, he said yes because he always says yes to you. This is part of the problem. "What kind of class?" was all he asked, and for a split second, you considered telling him the truth. "Self-defense," you said.

Now you and Frank take turns holding the skin taut and slicing in axial lines, as the manual instructs. Embalming fluid beads up, dribbles and leaks. An oily, wet darkness, Gracie's insides opening like burst fruit. The strangest thing isn't cutting someone open, you think, but the fact that mostly, *mostly*, people stay intact—that they move through their days unpunctured, that they don't go spilling out all the time.

When Jeremiah says that not everyone will get all the way to the heart, you look at Frank across the table. "But *we* will," you say. Frank nods as if he can see it in your face: this is what you came for, this is the whole thing. The black hole in your chest, the unseeable thing you have to see.

"Darling," says Frank, "we're about to start on the axilla now." He's talking not to you, but to Gracie. You're supposed to do this. You're supposed to talk to your corpse. But though you've now touched and prodded and manhandled a corpse, though you've now posed and Sharpied and sliced a corpse, this is the one thing you cannot, will not do.

Gracie's face, when you finally manage to look at it, is a kind of blankness you've never seen. Like she's just had the fright of her life and exited swiftly from her skin. It's not such a simple thing, you realize, to stand above a dead body, knife in hand, and feel completely blameless in the whole affair.

Jeremiah pauses at your table, registers the movement of your hands. "You can press harder," he says, resting a blue-gloved hand on yours. You feel yourself go stiff, but the scalpel moves certain and sure, and the membrane separates: a clean, straight line. "See?" says Jeremiah. "*Talk* to her while you do it."

"I will," you lie. "I will." You picture a satellite bouncing signals into empty space, your voice naked and undone. If anything, you'd like to apologize, though for what you're not exactly sure. Your brain whispers half-maniacally, half-sincere: *I'm sorry. I'm sorry for killing you.*

•

At night, you run. This is what you do. Is it the best or wisest thing to run through the dark streets of Canarsie late at night? Probably not. But you're beginning to believe there are no good or bad things, only better and worse things.

In your headphones, it's Prince the whole way through. Prince or whatever symbol he's known by. You too would like to slip from your body, from your name, alight into something formless and unspeakable. *See that body contorting on the stage—nameless, otherworldly—that isn't me; that's just the shimmering, pelvic-thrusting illusion through which I slip.*

Headlights of passing cars chase your shadow up the street. Running at night, you become a shadow, a lurker, a darkness peering into windows. You stare into small square scenes set aglow: people cooking and yelling and laughing, voices calling from room to room. You run and lurk and peer all the way home.

Home is the fifth-floor walkup you share with your cousin Georgie. Over a year ago, you emailed to ask if he knew any cheap sublets in the city. You were graduating into what was just beginning to be called the Great Recession, and Vik offered only the most minimal of part-time salaries. What you lacked in compensation and benefits, he said, you'd gain in exposure—a word that strikes you now as ridiculous and a little prophetic.

But Georgie, who you barely knew, surprised you. "Stay here," he wrote. "Granddad would be happy to have another writer in the apartment."

You hadn't understood quite how literal this would be—*another* writer—until you arrived and found your dead great-uncle's clothing still folded in every drawer, his possessions amassed in giant heaps: old shoes, filled-in crossword books, expired medications. The apartment all but frozen in time since his death.

For years, your great-uncle had been a gambler and a drunk, but late in life he sobered up and became a poet. You never really knew him—there'd been a split in the family—but now you like to stare up at the giant smoke stains above the bathtub and imagine him lying there, composing lines of poetry in his head.

Truthfully, the apartment is a wreck. Heaps of wayward possessions and every free surface covered with Diet Pepsi cans. Georgie drinks through boxes a week and leaves the cans stacked like strange modern sculptures. Mice have eaten through the cabinets, and a dust you pray isn't toxic sifts gently through holes in the ceiling.

The plan was for you to stay a few months, but already it's been over a year, poor Georgie sleeping on the couch. He is big and the couch is small, but when you offered to sleep there instead, he said he liked sleeping in front of the TV.

Sometimes you catch yourself avoiding Georgie. He's awkward and shy and speaks in halting, three-word sentences. Unless of course he's talking about wrestling, in which case he can go on and on. More than once you've found yourself trapped in the hall for hours as he narrated the long list of things one body can do to another on pay-per-view WWE. His best and only friend is a wiry cable repairman who comes over to watch wrestling and likes to fling racist epithets at the TV. At first you tried to argue with the cable repairman. Then you hid in your room. "That doesn't bother you?" you once asked Georgie, whose dad is Dominican. But Georgie only smiled bashfully and shrugged.

All night, the TV plays, shiny bodies punting one another across the ring. By now, you can recite all their names. You hear the announcers in your sleep.

You're still slick and shiny from running when you rewind the latest of the latest of the guru's tapes. His odd voice singsongs: *It's an office activated by the masters of time.* You wonder: is there such a thing as a spiritual office? All you can picture is the shabby and windowless office you share with Vik—an office so tiny he notes your lackluster response to bouncing Adobe icons, so cramped you can smell his sweat.

But the guru is talking about the offices of Khidr, a wandering green prophet. Or maybe he's only dressed in green—the guru can be hard to understand. *On the verge of losing this life, the aspirant goes through the desert-like regions, up through mountains. There is no way out. His offices are there.*

Sometimes you feel yourself growing to like the guru. On one recording, he told a long story about a cow who'd followed him all afternoon. You kept waiting for some sort of spiritual punch line, some tidy summation, but it never came—he just liked the cow. Later, he explained that dying was a joyful thing because the body was the excrement of the soul and everyone felt joyful while expelling excrement. After a car accident in 1979, he stopped speaking and spent the last decade of his life in silence.

You too can fall easily into long silences. It wouldn't be so terrible, you think, to never have to speak, to use only an alphabet board to communicate, as the guru did in his final years.

You're still transcribing when Danny calls. He's thirty-one, nine years older than you, but still there's something that goes oddly soft and boyish in his voice when he calls late at night, which is mostly when he calls.

"I smell like a dead person," you say when he asks you to come over.

"So?" You can hear him smiling his drunken smile. "What else is new."

Later, in his bed, you're quiet even for you, barely speaking except for one-word answers.

"Are you okay?"

"Yes."

"Do you want me to stop?"

"Yes."

"Isn't it good I ask you all these questions?"

You still haven't had sex. Most nights, you drink cheap whiskey and pass out next to each other. But then other nights, like this one, you think it will finally happen. You'll kiss him and hold onto his shoulders, and when he reaches for a condom, you won't push him away.

But always there's the ghost that rises up from the pit of your abdomen, stiffens in your limbs. Your arms aren't your arms anymore, moving as of a will all their own—a kind of zombie strength startling inside you.

Danny hands you a Valium. The first night, the night you met him at a bar, you froze beside him in bed, fear wrapping its hands around your throat. A long minute passed, and then finally you could breathe again. Danny looked at you and said, "Were you molested or something?"

You rolled your eyes. You weren't about to do this. Weren't about to be the kind of trembly girl always appearing on TV—a girl divulging secrets, a special victim.

So Danny reached into his bedside drawer and pulled out a pill. "Valium," he said, and then it became a kind of ritual between you. Sometimes you don't even swallow these pills, slipping them quietly into your bag, and yet you keep up the pretense—this give and take, this vaguely palliative gesture. You wonder if it's the only real thing that's ever happened between the two of you.

Tonight, you swallow the Valium and feel yourself drifting into someplace that's not quite sleep, passing over a long strange desert, rising up into mountainous air. And you think again how strange it is that people's outlines mostly stay intact, even when you lie very close to someone. Even then.

2.

    "How was your defense class?" asks Vik.

    "Self-defense," you correct him. "It was all right."

    "And are you defended now?" This is supposed to be a joke.

    "Yes," you say with faux gravity. "Watch out."

Vik is a paunchy man in his fifties with a graying goatee—a new development. "I'm going for a Salman Rushdie look," he told you some weeks ago. "Pre or post-hiding?" you asked. This was why you got to him, he said, touching your elbow a second too long.

You and Vik are on an upswing in the cycle. There have been weeks full of lighthearted office banter, of humorous-but-professional weekend anecdotes. But this also means that soon, very soon, Vik will lean across his desk and tell you how his wife hasn't had sex with him in years. Or he'll find a way to stand next to you at one of the nightly cocktail parties on the eighth floor, and after the toasts and speeches, after the candlelight dims, he'll press his hand to yours under the table.

The first time it happened was at one of these cocktail parties, after a particularly rousing speech by Lula. Someone handed you a drink, and you could feel Vik watching you. Before you could fully register what was happening, his hand had brushed against your thigh. That was the moment you first felt it: the self that rose up out of you to watch. You felt not panic or anger but the dull throb of collusion. *Run!* a part of you shouted in your ear. But the spectator self only shrugged. *See what happens next.*

Always after these incidents, you're cold and formal, and Vik acts like a boss again: courteous, professional. But then eventually, you let your guard down, which is when the whole thing starts over.

How many times can you do this? Not long ago, you went to a temp agency—took the typing test and filled out all the forms. But every time they call to offer you an assignment—a law firm, a private equity fund—you picture the grand carpeted hallways and galactic assembly rooms, the little booths full of translators speaking quietly into machinery. You think of the article you still haven't written, and you just can't do it—you can't leave this world, not yet.

A thousand times you've rebuked yourself for being overly familiar with Vik, especially in the early days, when you stayed working at your desk late into the night, took his phone calls at all hours of the day. You're too passive, you think. Too accommodating. You're too pretty, too ugly. You're so ugly, you appear lonely and therefore desperate.

It would be easier if Vik were a monster, a *Lifetime* original predatory boss. But in many ways, he's been good to you—plucking your application out from the many and championing your every article. Letting you write anything you want so long as it falls within the magazine's broad purview: chronicling the terrible things that happen to people in geopolitically insignificant corners of the world. While every reporter in the UN chases down statements on the latest Mideast crisis, you attend near empty meetings on child marriage and fistulas. You write about wars in countries where war is never called *war*, only *conflict*. You call up neglected researchers so happy to talk to you they all but write your stories.

Except lately, something's gone awry: you've written nothing in months. Of course, you know what it is—knew, though you wouldn't admit it, from the start. It's the dead girls: the long and wide-ranging feature you're supposedly writing on the murder of girls and women. Every day, you spend hours scrolling through websites with dark backgrounds and strident fonts, sites that attempt to hobble together a piecemeal tally. *Femicide*, they call it. You read about the hundreds of bodies unearthed in Juarez, bodies strangled and torched and mutilated. You read about mob attacks in Algeria, about shootings at universities. You read about mass rape and fatal fistulas. You read about the seemingly isolated attacks on women and girls in their homes and on the street—women killed by strangers and husbands and family members, by johns and coworkers and ex-boyfriends. Your story, you think, will be a kind of genealogy branching out in all directions, piercing through the solid veneer of the world and revealing a slow but steady female apocalypse.

Your first dead girl was the older cousin of a girl in your sixth-grade class. One day in homeroom, she announced that her cousin had gone missing and then dissolved into tears. No one believed her—she was the kind of girl who liked to say things just for shock value. She'd also said that her cousin had been modeling in Italy, which was one outlandish thing too many. But then a week later, it was on the local news—the body unearthed from a south Florida swamp, hacked up and shoved in a suitcase. The boyfriend had confessed.

Still, you didn't think much of it. It was one of those things that happened, then passed. It wasn't until you started working at a domestic violence shelter in college that you began to think again about the ways women were killed. A woman was most likely to be murdered by her partner when she was attempting to leave—this was a fact repeated with near-religious conviction at the shelter. And yet even among the lefty older feminists you worked for, you never heard anyone call it a hate crime. You began to suspect that the term *domestic violence* was itself a coy euphemism, a cleaned-up gloss.

And the more you tally up figures, the more you see dead girls everywhere: on giant subway ads, in the news, anesthetized on countless hour-long TV dramas. It's all begun to feel to you like a single death, a single crime. When you try to picture the article in your mind, you see each body like a star in an impossibly big constellation. Someone just had to draw in the lines.

Except you can't write. You type hunched over your laptop late into the night, then delete everything you've written the next morning. In the light of day, it all seems not just terrible but misguided and vaguely obscene: the idea of making horror into sentences, of making sentences that rise to the level of art—which you have to admit, finally, is what you're after. All this, the transmuting of violence into beauty, seems unthinkable.

But today is different. Today the new intern arrives—the first intern Vik let you hire yourself. Her name is Jennifer, and when she appears in the office door, she's older than you expected—at least five years your senior and significantly louder. Her eye makeup is perfectly applied, and she says things like "It's a pleasure." Suddenly you feel very young.

After two hours of work, Jennifer stands up to announce in her loud voice that she's breaking for lunch. Vik casts a skeptical eye as she disappears down the hall. "She doesn't have the legs for that skirt," he sniffs, then turns back to his computer.

●

The skin comes off easiest, and then there's another layer just below, almost silvery in the light. ("You're shining today," Frank tells Gracie.) Getting through this is like scraping paint off a wall, slow and horrible. You feel like a burglar trying to break into a house with a vegetable peeler.

It's tedious enough that you and Frank start competing to come up with the best terms for bodies. Blood-gusher. Gut-lugger. Sack of meat. Frank was an English major long ago, and since then he's been a truck driver, a substitute teacher, a traveling salesman. He says he likes what he does now best. Bodywork, he calls it—a term that revolts you just a little.

Earlier, you and Frank managed to flip Gracie onto her back, and now you try to avoid looking at her face. But still you hear her narrating in your head. *Chapter One, In Which a Rolfer and a Madwoman Take Up the Knife, or: Afterlife Among the Barbarians.*

When Frank asks what you do, you think of your unwritten article. You think of the near-empty assembly rooms and speeches on fistulas. You think of all this and say you're a transcriber. Somehow this seems truer. Lately, everywhere you go, you seem to be observing the Earth's permutations from on high, transcribing its terrible and beautiful configurations, all the details of your daily life passing through you to some invisible page.

"Hey, will you look at that." Frank nods at Gracie's toenails. Chips of bright red nail polish gleam in the light.

It's the toenails, finally, that get to you. Not the slick ropes of Gracie's intestines, not the pickled sacks of her organs, but a few chips of toenail polish. How you can slip out of one world and into the next, the whole mad scramble of your life fading out behind you, but the bad paint job on your second toe —that's the thing that stays.

You look at Gracie and think: *What is inside you?* Flesh, teeth, marrow, bone. Dark hidden rooms. All the minutes and hours of Gracie's days. Imprinted on cells, beneath the skin: hours missing and not.

One night the second month of college, you woke with a stranger's face pressed close to yours. A body, knuckled and heavy. Your own limbs turned to lead. Or not *yours*, exactly—in the dark, you weren't a *you* yet, not even a *what*. Your mind reeled for something, anything, to latch onto. It took the grinding of a small eternity to understand *what* and *how* and later *when*.

Then you were on the cold floor, feeling for your underwear in the dark. When you didn't find it, you started to crawl. You crawled because your limbs had turned to fins—strange, severed appendages that wouldn't move right. You crawled down a green-tinted hall, down stairs. Everything felt like underwater. You crawled all the way back to your freshman dorm, and in the morning you told no one, because you weren't sure what there was to tell.

None of this makes you particularly remarkable or special, certainly not a special victim. You've engineered your life in such a way so as to always be looking at far worse things—worse acts of violence, worse moments of terror. And yet, a small part of your brain still insists that those hours made a split in you, that they opened up a kind of schism in time, sent you in two ways at once. When later you asked your friends what they remembered of that night, they said only that you'd looked happy, that they saw you dancing in the chaos of bodies. But you couldn't remember this dancing self, and you began to think that she must be somewhere else, somewhere outside you. In a distant city, maybe, or just a subway stop away—the kind of person who might throw elaborate dinner parties or paint giant canvases. Maybe you've seen her passing on the street.

What the guru says about time: that it's like skin. That in moments of great terror or beauty, it can stretch wide open, and that a person might slip through.

"Time bomb," says Frank, and you look up, jolted. "A body," he explains. "A body is a kind of time bomb."

The next table over is debating what the former inhabitants of these bodies might say about all of you. You hear Gracie, a newscaster now, in your head: *Bringing you live updates from Day Two of the ongoing Yogi Hostage Crisis.*

"Rest their souls," someone murmurs.

"Thank God there's no soul," a lanky man replies.

Frank turns and stares. "What exactly do you think moved these bodies around, then?"

The lanky man shrugs apologetically. "Chemistry."

"Neurons," you chime in. "Sparks."

Frank gives you a look like you've betrayed him. But as much as you'd like to believe in something—anything would do—you can't quite tip this desire over into belief. Which isn't to say you haven't imagined it. Which isn't to say you haven't pictured the burnished bright coals of your insides lighting you up or rising in embers above your head. How it would be to look down and think: *Oh, so this is what I was.*

If you could just cut yourself open, peel back your insides—all the little gates and alleys, the webbed tunnels of veins. The sweet-sour reek of it, the clenched fist of the heart—cut loose, says Jeremiah, it unfolds, unravels. If you could just see inside yourself, you might finally understand it, this person you've become.

Night keeps coming earlier. This weekend the clocks get set back. "That's good," muses Jeremiah, watching as the rest of you draw up the sheets. "We should always go out into darkness."

"Say goodnight, Gracie," says Frank.

"Goodnight, Gracie," you whisper.

•

On Saturday, a small cloud of flies appears, circling the apartment hallway. There's a voicemail from an unknown number on your phone. You listen to the first five seconds before snapping it shut. *This is the Brooklyn Community Health Clinic—*

Before you left the clinic, you changed your mind, made up a fake number, but somehow they've found you anyway. You're still staring at your phone when it vibrates in your hand. *Unknown caller.* What do they want from you? You answer and are about to say they have the wrong number when you hear a loud, familiar voice. "I just wanted to give you notice."

It's Jennifer, the intern, and she's quitting. A slow dread rises in your stomach as she tells you that after work on Friday she went with Vik to the cocktail party on the eighth floor. Out of nowhere, Vik announced: "I have to do something." Then he grabbed her face in his hands and kissed her on the mouth.

"I'm sorry" is all you can say. "I'm so sorry."

Jennifer says it's fine, that she wrote herself a letter of recommendation and had Vik sign it.

"If there's anything I can do," you murmur before hanging up. "Anything at all."

It's only some moments later that you fully understand: you are not too pretty, too ugly. Not too familiar or accommodating or lonely. For the briefest of seconds, it stings, your unspecialness. Then quickly it transmutes to rage, white-hot and moving up your face. It didn't have anything to do with you.

●

A month ago, there was a blood drive at the UN. Like everyone, you went down and sat in the metal chairs, began filling out the forms. Then you got to the line that stopped you: *HIV status.* And it occurred to you for the first time that you didn't know. You'd mostly avoided doctors, but the few times you wound up in front of one, you found yourself stumped by the question *Are you sexually active?* It all seemed impossible to explain: the night in college, the missing hours, whatever did or didn't happen.

Eventually you'd merely put it out of your mind—so far out of your mind, it barely existed at all. It became like a memory that belonged to someone else—a story relayed by a friend or a scene from a movie—connected by only the thinnest of threads to you and your life. But the blood drive unturned something, churned up the stiff ground of your insides. The black hole opened in your chest, and you lay awake at night suddenly aware of yourself as a body—the same body then and now.

Finally, you went to the clinic. But once you were sitting there, a nurse telling you to make a fist, it occurred to you that maybe you didn't want to know. Because maybe you were dying, and maybe you'd only made it this far by not knowing. Of course you knew this was unlikely, knew all the statistics. You knew the odds were small, infinitesimal. But still, you were probably dying.

The night sky, when you run, is bruised red and violet. Breath scrapes your throat.

What Prince says: *Dearly Beloved, we are gathered here today—*

But this seems too on point. You skip ahead to the wailing of "When Doves Cry." You run faster.

You run the distance of three subway stops, all the way to East Flat-bush, where Danny lives, though you don't go to his building. Sometimes when you run, you have visions of strange men leaping from the bushes and hacking you to pieces. It's an odd comfort to think there'd be someone nearby, not to save you from death but just to witness it—to witness your body dismembered and bleeding.

Then faintly, very faintly, you hear what sounds like a woman screaming. It's coming from somewhere in the distance, somewhere behind you. You keep running. There's another scream—it seems to be moving somehow through the dark. Finally, on the third scream, you turn around. But there's nothing there. You pull out your head-phones, and there's just the sound of you panting on the sidewalk, cars gliding past. It's only when you put your headphones back in that you understand: the scream is coming from inside them, from inside your own ears.

In eighth grade, a story spread around school about a girl who'd been raped by five high school boys. You never knew her name, but when you pictured it, at thirteen, you thought: *It wouldn't be the worst thing.* You pictured the girl getting up afterward, walking away. You thought how at least she'd get to walk away. *Not like you'd die.*

You'd forgotten all about this for many years, and it was only run-ning, late one night, that the girl came back to you. You think of her, this nameless girl, and you think of the scream dying in your ears. Everything you witness, you witness too late.

You're almost asleep when Danny calls, but still you go. His apartment is dark, and neither of you speak. It occurs to you that you don't know what you are to each other. You're not in love. Not strangers, not friends.

You're just two people falling asleep in the same bed. How many nights can you spend in the bed of another person without coming to know them at least a little? There must be some sort of limit, a rule.

You turn away to face the dark and feel yourself sliding toward sleep. "I think I'm dying," you say quietly. Because this is easier to say than what you truly believe, which is that you're already dead.

Wordlessly, Danny reaches across you and holds your wrist in his hand. You remember telling him once about your fear of hearts and veins, the blood moving through you invisibly. Now you fall asleep this way—you facing the dark and Danny holding onto your veins, like he's making sure they won't seep out in the night.

You've started to see Gracie in the moments just before you sleep— her strange, startled expression and blanched yellow skin. The scalpel moves like a silver fish inside your dreams.

3.

    By Monday morning, the walls are covered in flies. Your great-uncle's apartment has endured all other manner of infestation—ants, cockroaches, mice—but this is something else. The walls black and moving, alive. You stay hidden beneath a sheet in bed, only emerging to dash to the bathroom.

You Google exterminators. The cheapest is four hundred dollars. You have barely three hundred in your back account. You consider trying to hawk your stash of unswallowed Valiums, accruing in a little blue heap on your great-uncle's bureau. Instead, you call your mother, weeping.

"Put it on my credit card," she sighs, then goes to look for her purse. You weep harder, feeling like a little kid.

"There's something else," your mother says, because you're still crying and because sometimes she just knows. Your mother is a little crazy and also a drunk, but she's good in a crisis. It's only when there's no crisis that she doesn't know what to do with herself.

You tell her about Danny, about the ghost that rises from your abdomen. You tell her how you'll never have sex with anyone.

"Of course you will," says your mother. Nothing you've said seems to shock her. "You're much too sensual a person never to have sex with anyone." Then she asks: "Do you have a vibrator?"

"No." Suddenly you're not crying at all.

She tells you where to go online—the kind of pastel-infused website that refers to its merchandise as *wonders* and where every wonder has a name like Natural Contours Goddess. "Just practice on your own."

•

The exterminator tells you that flies like to descend en masse when something dead is holed up in the wall. "But these are everywhere," he says, baffled. You ask if it could be the Diet Pepsi cans. "Nah." He shakes his head. "That's stuff's all chemicals."

He goes around planting bright blue glue traps on every free surface. You can't believe this costs four hundred dollars.

You don't go to work and don't go to class. You don't call Vik to tell him you're not coming in. Instead, you make your bed a kind of makeshift fort, and inside it you sit very still. You dial your voicemail and listen to a stranger tell you calm and matter-of-factly that you're not dying, that there's nothing wrong with you. That all this has been for nothing.

What you should feel, you know, is relieved. *Weary*, you think. *That's what I feel.* Because if you're not dying, you must instead be living. You stare at your phone for a very long time.

●

When Georgie comes home from work, you tell him about the exterminator, and suddenly you're crying again. "I can't live like this," you say. "There's something dead in our walls." Even though this isn't exactly what the exterminator said.

Georgie does the same thing he always does. The same thing he did when you came to him about the cockroaches, the ceiling dust, the mice. He smiles abashedly at the floor and tells you it'll get better.

You're beginning to hate Georgie a little. You hate the stink and filth of the apartment—the piles of crusted dishes, the spray of little black hairs in the bathroom sink—and how he refuses to get rid of a single thing, every closet and drawer crowded with a dead man's possessions. You hate the way he's stuck—so stuck, he's paralyzed.

"It *won't* get better," you say. Now you're sobbing. You're not a crier, but already you've wept twice today, like some great storm has come and flooded your insides.

"Look," Georgie says quietly. "Just look."

And then you see he's right. The flies have thinned. The walls have surfaced. They're no longer moving, grimed only with dirt. Together, you and Georgie go around the apartment and shake glue traps into garbage bags. You ask about the latest wrestling match and listen as Georgie tells you the long history of the Undertaker, his feuds and personas and what his comeback might mean.

4.

On the last day of class, Frank takes a bone saw to Gracie, apologizing all the while. In a flash, Gracie jerks forward, spits something across the room. Your heart thuds in your chest. Practically the whole rooms leaps. There's a moment of stunned silence, and then everyone laughs: it's her dentures.

By now, says Jeremiah, you can start to see the ways people have died. How their organs blackened and festered. How they grew their deaths inside them.

On the last of the guru's tapes you transcribed—the last of his tapes, you realize now, you'll ever transcribe—the guru claimed to know the future. It wasn't by magic or premonition, he insisted, but that for him time had grown very wide. *In the light of the future, everything has already happened.*

You pull at a strand of yellowed tissue, gristly and veined. If this were a movie, you think, this is the point where you'd be treated to flashbacks of Gracie's life—a montage of her days and years, sped up toward their inevitable end. You'd see her drinking from a flask at work or chain-smoking secretly in the night. You'd see her death—maybe slow, maybe sudden. Maybe strangled with a pair of stockings.

But you see nothing. Frank says maybe it was her heart, which peeks out now from the depths, ugly and stiff.

Rush, rush, rush, you hear in your ear. Because you and Frank are close, so close. The surrounding tissue is thick and fibrous, and together you fall into a silent rhythm, cutting and unwinding. It's only when the scalpel clatters to the table that you see Frank's hands are trembling. "I'm fine," he tells you. "I just get the shakes sometimes. It's a condition."

Slowly, the heart emerges in full—a brown and muscled thing the size of your fist. Frank does a low whistle. "It's dumb to get sentimental about an organ, I know, but what can you do?"

Inside you, you feel it: something unraveling in your chest. You look down to steady yourself, glance around the room. How unlikely, you think—you don't know any other word for it—how unlikely you're all here, down in the heart of the mortuary basement, cutting into what used to be a person. Or maybe this is just what you do, what you do and must go on doing all your life. The most likely thing in the world: diving into another person. Diving and diving for the thing that might save you.

Frank's hands are shaking worse now, and you see that you're going to have to do this last part on your own. And you see too, as if by the wide and astonished light of the future, that you'll never go back to your job at the UN, never walk its grand carpeted halls. You won't give notice, won't return Vik's calls. You see a future of coffee runs for hedge fund analysts, of typing up memos and law briefs. And you see, of course, what you already knew: that you'll never finish your story on dead girls, the one that was supposed to rise up above the face of the Earth, draw in the lines of an impossible constellation.

But for now, there's only the heart, dumb and unmoving. There's only the cut you have to make. Your voice, when you hear it, surprises you.

"Come on, Gracie. Come on, you blood-gusher, you gut-lugger, you shining sack of meat. Just this one last thing."

NOTES

"Houses" quotes from Alexandra David-Néel's translation of the Bardo Thödol in *Immortality and Reincarnation*.

In "Coming To," the quote from the witness to the Loudun trial is taken from Michel de Certeau's *The Possession at Loudun*. "There was darkness all over my face" is a quote from "Explaining the Factory Faintings" in *The Cambodia Daily*. I am also indebted to the work of Devon Hinton.

"Your Village Has Been Bombed" is the title of a leaflet described by Jonathan Schell in *The Military Half*.

"Choreograph" quotes from Vaslav Nijinsky's diaries, Bronislava Nijinska's *Early Memoirs*, and Doris Humphrey's *The Art of Making Dances*.

In "Nausicaa," the line "It was an affair that could only exist in the violence of trench warfare, with death always nearby" is taken from the film *Jules et Jim*.

ACKNOWLEGMENTS

Infinite gratitude:

To the magazines and editors who first published these stories (or early incarnations of these stories): Adeena Reitberger and Rebecca Markovits; Sven Birkerts, Jennifer Alise Drew, and Bill Pierce; Carolyn Kuebler and Josh Tyree; Kwame Dawes, Ashley Strosnider, and Sarah Fawn Montgomery; Andrew Malan Milward; Joseph Langdon and Brett Finlayson.

To Michelle Dotter, wisest and most insightful of editors, and to Dan Wickett, Guy Intoci, Michael Seidlinger, and everyone at Dzanc for tirelessly tugging this book into the world.

For time and space: the University of Southern California and the University of Missouri-Kansas City.

To teachers, mentors, guides: Christie Hodgen, Dana Johnson, Aimee Bender, Hadara Bar-Nadav, Michelle Boisseau, Anthony Shiu, Whitney Terrell, Michael Pritchett, Deb Gorlin, Janalynn Bliss.

To friends and readers across many times and places: Lauren Hart, Dene Chen, Bridget Di Certo, Leanna Bales, Flannery Cashill, Andrew Johnson, the Phnom Penh Writers' Group, the Kansas City coven.

To my family, who contributed in ways big and small: Dale Carlson-Bebout, John Bebout, Lauren Daniels, Jo Ann Jecko, Gabe Benitez, Bill Carlson. My parents: Neil and Joan, ports in the storm; Karen and Jeffrey, believers from the start. My sisters, the earliest constellations of my imagination. My brothers, who helped me dream it up.